"Dinosaurs," Raymond ⟨⟩ staring at the creatures in the distance.

"I can't believe it," Hugh said, astonished. "I just can't believe it! They're so—so—"

"Big!" Raymond said.

"Right! Ain't nothin' alive stands that tall. Nothin', I tell ya!"

Raymond stiffened as a thought struck him. "Hugh...do you believe in the hereafter?"

"Why?"

"The dinosaurs died out ages ago. If they're here, then maybe we died too! Maybe this is *heaven!*"

Suddenly a rustling came from the brush behind the boys. A pink and yellow creature emerged. The calf-size dinosaur started making squawking sounds. They made no sense at first. Then the boys realized that the dinosaur was actually *speaking* to them.

"Not heaven, though some think it so," she said. "I am Bix. Welcome you are. Welcome you both are. Welcome to Dinotopia."

VISIT THE EXCITING WORLD OF

IN THESE BOOKS:

Windchaser by Scott Ciencin

River Quest by John Vornholt

Hatchling by Midori Snyder

Lost City by Scott Ciencin

AND COMING SOON:

Sabertooth Mountain by John Vornholt

DINOTOPIA
WINDCHASER

by Scott Ciencin

BULLSEYE BOOKS

Random House 🏠 New York

*I'm very proud that this novel, which came so much from the heart,
is the first to be dedicated to my beloved wife, Denise.
You are my heart, my soul, my reason to live. I love you, sweetheart.
Thank you for all you've given me.
Also, heartfelt thanks to Alice Alfonsi and Jim Thomas of Random House,
editors and friends extraordinaire, and to James Gurney,
for throwing open the gates and allowing me to enjoy myself so much
in his wonderful playground. Read on, Macduff!
—S.C.*

*Special thanks to
paleontologist Michael Brett-Surman, Ph.D.,
James Gurney, and Scott Usher.*

A BULLSEYE BOOK PUBLISHED BY RANDOM HOUSE, INC.

Copyright © 1995 by James Gurney.
Cover art copyright © 1995 by James Gurney.
All rights reserved under International and Pan-American Copyright Conventions.
Published in the United States by Random House, Inc., New York,
and simultaneously by Random House of Canada Limited, Toronto.
Based on *Dinotopia*® by James Gurney,
published in 1992 by Turner Publishing, Inc., Atlanta.
All rights reserved.

Library of Congress Catalog Card Number: 94-67485

ISBN: 0-679-86981-6

RL: 5.8

Manufactured in the United States of America 10 9 8 7 6 5 4

DINOTOPIA IS A REGISTERED TRADEMARK OF THE GREENWICH WORKSHOP, INC.,
© 1992 JAMES GURNEY

Cover illustration by Michael Welply

WINDCHASER

CHAPTER 1

September 20, 1863

Raymond Wilks sat on his bed, nervously handling his father's pocketwatch. He didn't have to look at its face to know the time. It was exactly one minute later than the last time he'd checked.

The thirteen-year-old waited alone in the cold, tiny cabin on the prison ship *Redemption*. His father was the ship's surgeon. More than an hour ago, he was called above deck.

A storm raged, and lightning flashed through the porthole behind Raymond. Fists of hail beat against the glass in a furious rhythm. Shadows danced, and thunder rocked the walls. The cabin rose and fell, following the motions of the ship on the crashing waves.

The ship had sailed from London. It was bound for the penal colonies of Western Australia with a load of dangerous criminals. Days ago, the terrible storm had begun and blown the ship wildly off course. Today, the prisoners had taken advantage of the chaos and risen up against the crew.

All through the *Redemption*, a battle was raging. The prisoners were attempting to take control of the ship!

Suddenly, a shot rang out from the hall. Raymond shuddered as he heard a thump that sounded like a fallen body. The howls of angry men drifted close.

Another flash of lightning lit his cabin. Raymond saw his reflection in the glass of his extinguished reading lamp. A shock of brown hair fell across his forehead, and a haunted look crept into his wide blue eyes.

People often told Raymond how much he looked like his father. He had the same serious brow with the same strong, confident features in the making. But now Raymond could no longer see the resemblance. All he saw was his own terror.

Fighting back tears, Raymond felt ashamed of himself. He was acting like a child.

Before Stephen Wilks left, he gave his son strict orders to remain in their cabin with the door bolted shut until the trouble passed. Yet Raymond desperately wanted to run and find someone to tell him everything would be all right. He wanted his father to return to the cabin and calm him with his gentle smile.

A great wave caught the ship. Raymond cried out as the cabin lurched forward. The boy was tossed out of bed, onto the hard wood floor. He felt like a fledgling being hurled from the nest. Gathering his courage, Raymond rose to his knees and listened for a moment. The sounds in the corridor stopped.

The ship righted itself, sending Raymond sliding back into a wooden chest. He grabbed hold of it for support and hauled himself to his feet. The pocketwatch slipped from his hand. He picked it up and dropped it into his boot—a trick of his father's. Raymond had seen him do this whenever they traveled through dark or dangerous terrain.

Raymond had once asked him, "Father, why not hide your money clip in your boot instead? If it's thieves you're worried about—"

"Money can be replaced," Stephen Wilks had told his son. "Let them have the money, and perhaps they will search no further. This watch is special because of the memories attached to it. My father gave it to me the day I became a physician. And one day I will give it to you."

"*If* I become a healer."

His father had laughed. "No matter what path you choose, I will *always* be proud of you."

A little more than an hour ago, his father pressed the pocketwatch into Raymond's hands. A sad look came into the older man's eyes when Raymond asked why he was being given the keepsake now.

"Just hold it for me," his father said with a gentle smile. "I'll be back for it. You'll see."

But he did not come back.

Now, more than an hour later, Raymond was

going to find him. After taking in a deep breath, he unbolted the lock, eased open the door, and peered into the corridor.

Raymond could see nothing. The hall was shrouded in darkness. The lanterns that usually hung along the wall had either been taken or smashed.

Raymond's knees became watery. A tightness formed in his stomach. He forced himself to think only of his father, then he left the cabin. He used the wall to guide him, and soon reached a ladder that would take him above deck.

He climbed to the top rung and stopped.

The trap door above him was closed. It took all of his strength to force it open. Icy wind and rain struck his face. He nearly lost his grip on the ladder. His flailing hand fell upon a coiled rope near the opening to the main deck. With determination born of fear, Raymond grabbed hold and pulled himself up.

The storm was worse than he imagined. He could see little more than a few feet before him. When he tried to stand, Raymond slipped on the slick hard wood of the deck. The breath was drummed out of him.

Above the rising wail of the wind, he heard pistol shots and the crashing of swords. Suddenly, a figure appeared before him.

"It's the Wilks lad!" someone shouted.

"Come to join the party, has he?" another asked. The second man's malevolent tone robbed Raymond of any hope that these men were crew members.

Raymond tried to scramble out of the path of the approaching figures, but his efforts were wasted. Someone else grabbed him from behind. He was hauled to his feet, his arms pinned behind his back.

A man carrying a lantern came forward. Pockmarks covered his face, and his eyebrows were a single line across his forehead. Long scraggly hair and an ill-kept beard framed his hard features.

"Greetings, son of Stephen Wilks, *former* ship's surgeon," the bearded man shouted over the storm. "I wonder if *you* will give us as much trouble as your dear papa."

Did this mean that his father was dead? Raymond would not believe it! "Where is my father?" Raymond cried.

The bearded man grinned, revealing a mouth filled with rotted teeth. "Gone, lad. We threw his body overboard! Same as we're going to do to you." With that, Raymond was hauled toward the side of the ship.

Thunder roared, and lightning ripped across the sky. A single bolt broke into three jagged branches. For an instant, the ship was lit up as if the sun had miraculously appeared.

In that brief moment, Raymond saw the black and churning sea. He thought of his father's body sinking deeper, deeper into its bottomless depths.

This can't be happening, Raymond thought. His

father could not be dead! Raymond longed for a chance to touch him one more time. But even that had been denied him.

"*Father!*" Raymond cried into the wind.

The bearded man grabbed Raymond's arm and hauled him to the rail. "Since you seem so intent on being close to your dear papa, I think I'll send you right where he's gone!"

Suddenly, before Raymond could be tossed into the sea, another figure leaped out of the storm. A heavy wooden object was brought down upon the bearded man. He sank to the deck, his lantern crashing and going out.

In the sudden darkness, Raymond felt a sharp wind rip past his left ear. The man who had been holding him from behind cried out and loosened his grip.

As lightning flashed across the sky again, Raymond saw a tall, thin young man standing over the body of the bearded convict. Raymond was startled to see that his savior was also a prisoner, and only a few years older than Raymond!

"These bloody fools can't see what's coming," the black-haired stranger said as he grasped Raymond's arm and pulled him toward the rail.

"But we can't—" Raymond protested weakly. He could not believe it! Had this boy saved him only to send him to the same watery grave? But then, in the distance, Raymond saw a high gray wall racing their way.

The young prisoner was lean but strong. He gripped Raymond around the waist and launched both of them over the side. An instant later they struck the hard, churning waters, and vanished beneath them.

CHAPTER 2

The water was cold. Raymond broke the surface alone, gasping for breath. The older boy was floating beside him. For a minute, Raymond feared he would look back at the ship and see prisoners pointing their pistols at him. But when he turned, he saw something even more terrifying.

A huge, gray wave towered over the ship. It seemed to hesitate. On the ship's deck, most of the men looked stunned. A few ran toward the rail.

"Swim, blast ya!" yelled the black-haired boy.

Raymond tried to force his paralyzed limbs into motion, but his mind was shutting down in the face of certain death. There was no point in trying to swim from here. The wave would be upon them before they were a hundred yards from the ship.

With a cry of frustration, the older boy grabbed the back of Raymond's shirt collar and began to swim away. Flipping over, Raymond started to kick. He swam with a fury matched only by the young prisoner who had dragged him from the ship.

"That's it, that's right, come on!" the older boy cried. "Put your back into it, if ya want to live!"

Raymond did as he was commanded.

I don't want to die, he thought. *I want to live. I want to make all my father's sacrifices mean something. I want to live!*

Suddenly, several shapes appeared in the water beside the swimmers. They were dark and sleek, with fins that cut smoothly through the rough waves.

Raymond's heart nearly stopped. Was he now going to become the main dish for two hungry sharks?

Then one of the shapes raised its head. Raymond gasped with relief as he looked into the noble face of a dolphin!

One of the dolphins glided beneath Raymond and rose up toward him, its fin suddenly appearing between his hands.

Extraordinary. Impossible. The dolphin seemed set on saving Raymond! Looking over, Raymond saw the other boy grab hold of the second dolphin's fin. Raymond quickly did the same. The dolphin's flesh was warm, despite the cool temperature of the ocean waters.

Behind him, Raymond heard the great wave crash down upon the ship. The sound rose above the endless drumming rain and churning waves. Raymond knew it would be a matter of only seconds before he felt the wave's impact and was buried beneath the waters.

But suddenly, he was racing forward at a great speed. He felt the crush of water falling upon him, but by now he was clear of all but the tail end of the wave.

For a moment he and the dolphin were sent many feet below. In no time they were rising upward again, back to the surface. The currents created by the huge wave continued to propel them forward.

Raymond held on, though what little energy he had was now all but wasted. One hand gripping the fin, the other wrapped around the dolphin's body, Raymond closed his eyes and hoped he would live to see daylight.

Some time later—hours, minutes, there was no way to tell—Raymond caught sight of a number of breakers. The other boy whooped and yelled, letting go of his dolphin and swimming toward the rocks.

The storm was lessening. In the rare flashes of lightning, Raymond saw the white sand of a shoreline.

"Thank you," he whispered, then let go of the dolphin who had carried him to safety.

Moments later Raymond was climbing onto the rocks and grasping the arms of his rescuer. Together, they found their way to shore.

They both collapsed in exhaustion as a deep, dreamless sleep overcame them.

Raymond felt warmth seeping into him. It was wonderful! His eyes flickered open, and the glare of sunlight blinded him.

He rolled onto his side and stretched. The fine sand beneath him felt soft under his awakening body.

He yawned and, for a moment, even felt happy to be alive. Then thoughts came flooding back. He remembered the ship and his murdered father.

Raymond sat up. He wiped the sleep from his eyes and looked around him. Clear blue ocean waves gave way to the long, white sand beach. Beyond lay a dense green forest.

On the beach, several yards away, was a black-haired boy wearing what was left of a prisoner's uniform. He was leaning on his elbows, staring out to sea. Raymond followed his gaze and was immediately taken by an odd vision.

Several dolphins raced back and forth, diving and bursting from the water. To Raymond, they seemed to perform a kind of aquatic ballet. The sight was both dazzling and strange.

"Don't bloomin' believe it," the older boy said with a thick lower-class London accent. "But I *think* they been waitin' to see ya was all right. All this hubbub started when ya come 'round."

"Uh huh," Raymond said, disoriented.

The older boy made his hand into a fist and showed the back of it to Raymond. "Quick! How many fingers am I holdin' up?"

"That's not funny," Raymond said as he rose to his feet and stretched.

"Says who?"

The older boy looked back to the dolphins playing in the waters. He was thin and pale from his time in dark cells and the *Redemption*'s hold. Nevertheless, he appeared quite strong, with curly black hair, bright green eyes, and sharp features. Though his clothes were torn, this boy gave off the pride and confidence of a prince.

Turning, Raymond looked toward the forest behind them. The flora was odd. Exotic, even. Though he was well traveled, he had never seen anything quite like it.

Something that looked like a pine cone the size of a man was plainly visible. Ferns grew from its crest. The trees were like palms, only stranger somehow—taller, fiercer. He was certain he spied oversized magnolias and ginkgos.

"The name's Hugh O'Donovan, in case ya was wonderin'."

The older boy's words yanked Raymond away from his observations. Raymond looked over to his companion. "My name is—"

"Raymond Wilks. Yeah, I know. Your father was a good man. I'm sorry."

The thirteen-year-old turned his gaze downward. Tears began to choke him, and Raymond tried to hold them back. He did not want to cry in front of his new friend.

Then panic struck him. He yanked off his boot and turned it upside down. The pocketwatch tumbled out. Raymond clawed it from the cool sand and held it close.

The watch had stopped—just like his father's heart. He pulled it away and stared at the cracked surface.

"What's that?" Hugh asked.

"My father gave it to me," Raymond said.

The older boy nodded and said nothing more.

"You saved my life," Raymond said.

"Yeah. So?"

"I just—I wanted to say thank you."

Hugh shrugged. An awkward silence followed. The dolphins finished their celebration and swam off. Hugh raised a hand in a slight wave.

Finally, Raymond asked, "Do you think anyone else survived?"

"I doubt anyone else had the brains to jump ship in time." Hugh paused in thought, then added, "A lot o' good men died last night."

"Yes, the captain was very kind and—"

"I was talkin' about the bloke I was chained up with."

Raymond slipped the watch back into his boot. "Really?"

"Uh huh. Harry, he said his name was. Ya know what wicked crime he was payin' for?"

Raymond shook his head.

"Stealin' bread to feed his children. Odd part is, if he'd been fat and slow, they would've let him off! But

13

Harry was young and strong—a real good worker—so he was put on the ship. Like me."

"But that's not fair," said Raymond. "Why should a man's sentence be decided by whether or not he's a 'good worker'?"

"Because the English crown has a bloomin' new pact with the Aussies, that's why!"

"Pardon?"

"The Australians. They need cheap workers, see?"

"Did your friend tell you all this?" Raymond asked. "The man you were chained up with?"

Hugh nodded. "The Aussies started all these townships out in the bloody boonies, way on the other side of the continent from their big cities in the east. So they need cheap workers to man their work camps and help build the west colonies up, y'see?"

"I see," Raymond said.

"No, ya don't. There's this huge wilderness beyond the work camps. I was told most o' the guards don't even bother postin' sentries. If the prisoners go into the wild, so be it. Either they come back or they starve."

"Ah," Raymond said.

"I'm sayin' all this 'cause I fear we may have landed right where we was bound."

Raymond nodded, despair washing over him. "Australia."

"Question is, what part. Are we near the cities, where we might have a chance, or right in the middle o' that bloody unfriendly wilderness?"

Both of them looked to the forest.

Hugh shrugged. "I don't see much o' anythin' that looks like a city."

"You could be wrong," Raymond said weakly. He felt despair and fear closing in on him. "This might not be Australia."

"True. But if we're on some uncharted island, I don't guess our chances are much greater—"

Raymond was unable to contain his tears any longer. He sat down heavily and buried his face in his hands.

"Hey, now," Hugh said. "None of that."

"S-s-sorry," Raymond said between racking sobs. "But what are we going to do? We don't know where we are, there's no one here, how are we going to *survive?* I've always had my father around. Now he's gone!"

Hugh sighed. "Come on, now. It's not *that* bad."

"But you just said—"

"Goes to show I don't always think before I open me trap. All right then?"

Raymond's face was flushed. Tears streaked down from his reddened eyes.

Hugh got up, tore a strip of cloth from his sleeve, and passed it to Raymond. "Here, dry yourself off, why don'tcha?"

The younger boy almost laughed, despite his tears. He took the cloth and blew his nose.

"Now I bloody well don't want it back," Hugh said.

Raymond laughed again. Hugh knelt down and helped the boy to his feet. Raymond was a little wobbly.

"You need some food in ya, that's what ya need," Hugh said.

"Where are we going to find any?" Raymond asked.

Hugh pointed to the woods. "Looks like some kind o' trail to me. With any luck, it's man-made. And not Western Australian man-made, either."

"With any luck," Raymond said, his gaze returning to the waters.

"Unless you're an expert fisherman or somethin'?"

Raymond spun. "Not likely. I can't even swim very well. Lucky those dolphins saved us—"

"Bleedin' amazin', wannit?"

"It was!" Raymond said as they walked toward a gap between two great trees. "I read somewhere that dolphins were intelligent, but this defies all reason!"

"I know," Hugh said, laughing. "Like the bleedin' circus, only with fins!"

Minutes later, they disappeared into the trees.

CHAPTER 3

The two boys walked deep into the forest, marveling at all they saw.

Odd-looking birds with brilliantly colored plumage flew past them while a group of salamanders crossed their trail. Occasionally, an animal screech or cry made them jump.

When Hugh saw an oversized fruit dangling from a tree, he stopped. Before Raymond knew what was happening, his friend leaped into the air and plucked it from its branch.

"That might be poisonous," Raymond cried out as Hugh took a bite.

"Right," Hugh said, chomping away until he finished a mouthful. "Tell that to me stomach. I don't know 'bout you, but I haven't seen much of anythin' that looks familiar."

Raymond nodded slowly.

"So the only way to see if somethin'll hurt us is to try it, eh?"

"I suppose."

Hugh plucked another fruit. It was dark red and shiny. If it had been a bit smaller, it could have passed for an apple. Hugh tossed the fruit to Raymond. "We'll wait a while, see if I keel over. If not, we'll figure it's safe."

Raymond sighed. "Okay."

"We're gonna have to toughen you up a bit, now aren't we?" Hugh said cheerily. "See, I ain't *never* had anyone to take care o' me. I had to learn the ins an' outs o' survivin' all by meself. But don't worry. I'll teach ya. We've come this far together—I'm not about to give up on ya now!"

Raymond smiled. His stomach was growling, but his mind made him wait a good ten minutes before he bit into the fruit. The tangy taste was strange to him, yet quite good.

They quickly came upon a hard-packed dirt road that was certainly man-made. It was twice as wide as any road Raymond had ever seen.

The boys decided to stick to this road. Once in a while, they paused to inspect some strange tracks. Some were made by wheels, others by creatures that left shallow, dusty footprints larger than an elephant's!

"Raymond?" Hugh asked.

"Yes?"

"You're an educated lad."

"I suppose," Raymond said.

"How *big* would a creature have to be to leave tracks like that?" Hugh wondered.

"You don't want to know."

Hugh grimaced. "You're right, I don't."

Raymond bent low. "This really is quite amazing."

Hugh shrugged. "Probably just a prank or somethin' played by some o' the locals."

Raymond nodded in agreement, but his brow creased in thought.

"Bloomin' odd place, this," Hugh said. "Truly, truly, truly *odd*."

They resumed their travels and tried to ignore the appearance of more and more of the huge tracks. They finally stopped when they reached a fork in the road.

"Which way should we go?" asked Raymond.

Hugh grinned. "Left is right, and right is wrong. That's the rule I always follow."

They continued on, down the left fork, and watched the dense trees give way to rolling green pastures. The older boy was nervous when this happened.

Hugh was used to being ready to duck and run on short notice. The forest felt safer to him should they encounter trouble. There were many hiding places within the trees. But then he reminded himself that this land did have a civilization of some kind. And that meant *opportunity*.

"Raymond, you should know somethin'," Hugh said. "If there's a town o' some sort, we may not be all that welcome. Beggars rarely are. We may have no choice but to…ah…*liberate* a few things for our survival. Know what I mean?"

"Liberate?" asked Raymond. "You mean take—steal?"

Hugh shrugged.

"You were a thief, weren't you?" Raymond guessed.

Hugh winked. "Whatever gave you that idea?"

"How did you get caught?"

"If you're worried about me skills not bein' the best, you're wrong. Standing before you is—or was—the best pickpocket in all o' London. I was only brought down on account o' a bloke I thought was me friend. He turned me in for a reward. Bleedin' turncoat, he was."

"But you're just a kid, like me!"

Hugh shook his head. "I haven't been that since I was old enough for me parents to sell me into apprenticeship."

Suddenly, Hugh spotted a copse of trees upon a rise. He led Raymond to cover, then peered into the valley below.

"Not possible," Hugh muttered, his features becoming ashen. Raymond moved forward and gasped.

In the distance lay a long farmhouse of some sort, with a windmill at one end and an observation tower at the other. A vast orchard bordered the entire western stretch of the property.

Raymond and Hugh watched as a half-dozen people walked about. But it was the creatures standing

20

beside the men and women that made the boys gape in astonishment.

Gathered before the farm, seemingly set on some odd communion with the humans, was a troop of creatures that had no place in modern-day reality. They were all sizes and shapes, all colors. Each was adorned with some form of natural armament—spikes, raised scales, clubbed tails.

Some were as large as elephants, others as tall as towering oaks. A pair of man-size creatures stood on two legs and reminded Raymond of ostriches.

Raymond knew the word for this group of creatures. Just last summer his father had taken him to a display of fossils from creatures like these.

"Dinosaurs," Raymond whispered.

"I can't believe it," Hugh said. "I just can't believe it, that's all! They're so—so—"

"Big!" Raymond said.

"Right! Ain't nothin' alive stands that tall. Nothin', I tell ya!"

"But they *are* right in front of us."

"Stop remindin' me!"

"It looks like a delegation of some sort," Raymond said.

"Or a huntin' party," Hugh countered.

"Don't be absurd. Look at the way they get along with people. These creatures aren't out to hurt anyone."

"Wanna bet? I'll be happy so long as we don't end up in a dinosaur stew."

Raymond stiffened as another thought suddenly struck him. "Hugh…do you believe in the…in the hereafter?"

"Why?"

"The dinosaurs died out long ago. If they're here, and people are here, then maybe we died too! Maybe this is *heaven!*"

At that moment a rustling came from the brush behind the boys, causing both of them to whirl. Facing them was a creature the likes of which they'd never before seen.

Its rough skin was pink and yellow. The ridge above its eyes reminded Raymond of a woman's beret. But its birdlike beak and the tiny spikes protruding from its cheeks hardly looked feminine.

Compared to the behemoths in the valley, this creature was small, about the size of a calf. And it had an unmistakably gentle way about it.

The dinosaur opened its mouth and started making squawking sounds. They made no sense to Raymond at first. Then he realized the dinosaur was actually *speaking* to him.

"Not heaven, though some think it so," she said. "I am Bix. Breathe deep, seek peace. Welcome you are. Welcome you both are. Welcome to Dinotopia."

Slack-jawed, Hugh stared at the creature for a moment. Finally, he regained enough composure to mutter, "It's the fruit, that's what it is. It was poisoned. We're havin' feverish visions!"

The dinosaur sighed as if she had been through this before. "For centuries we have had visitors from your many lands."

"I should have listened when ya said it might be poisoned," Hugh said to Raymond. "That's always been my problem—I never listen."

"You're not listening *now*," Raymond said.

"True," Hugh said. "There's a reason."

Bix laughed. "Come with me. I will introduce you to Nicolai and the others."

"I don't think so," Hugh said.

Raymond touched his friend's arm. "Hugh, if we don't go with her, what are we going to do?"

"I dunno, but—"

Bix angled her head slightly. "If I am not real, what harm can come from following me?"

"Um…ah—" Hugh stammered. "We might be walkin' off a cliff or somethin'!"

"Pardon?" Bix said.

"Like a bunch o' sleepwalkers!" Hugh said. "We can't trust our eyes!"

"Yes," Bix said. "I can see how that might make life difficult."

Raymond was struggling not to become overwhelmed by the odd sights before him. Hugh's attitude was not helping any. "I'm going. If you won't come, I can't make you."

Hugh nodded. "All right, I'll go. Why not? We'll get eaten instead of gettin' something to eat."

23

Bix cocked her head again, as if thinking. "If you are right, and we dinosaurs are not real, you have little to fear. How can you be eaten by something that does not exist?"

"I—" Hugh began, then shook his head, giving up on trying to figure it all out. "All right, then. Off we go."

CHAPTER 4

The trio walked down the rise, in plain view of the dinosaurs and humans standing by the windmill.

"I'm afraid only a few will be free to speak with you," Bix said. "Noonfeast has just ended, and it is time to get back to work."

As they descended into the valley, Raymond found his attention drawn to the orchard. Men and women slipped into harnesses that fit around their shoulders and chests. Large curved handles reached a foot above and behind their heads. The long-neck dinosaurs, most of whom stood as tall as the mill, bit down on the handles. They lifted the humans high up to the fruit at the top of the trees.

The moment a picker retrieved a fruit, he was eased back toward the earth, where he dumped his prize into a cart. Another dinosaur, one that looked somewhat like a rhino, with a spike above the bridge of its nose and several in its crest, stood ready to drag the cart off when it was filled.

"What are those long-necks called?" Raymond asked.

"Brachiosaurus," Bix replied.

Raymond shook his head in amazement. "They work together. Humans and dinosaurs."

"Of course," Bix said. "There is no other way."

"Naturally," Hugh said, shaking his head.

They came closer to the farm. The ground vibrated when one of the larger dinosaurs closer to the mill padded this way or that. Far off to the left, Raymond observed fields. Dozens of humans and dinosaurs now toiled there.

A leathery smell came to Raymond. A man approached, flanked by two rose-colored dinosaurs twice his size.

"Newcomers!" Bix announced. "Dolphinbacks!"

"How'd ya know we was carried here by dolphins?" Hugh asked. "We never told ya!"

"I think it's common here," Raymond said. He looked down at Bix. "Or am I wrong?"

"Not wrong," she said. "Bright boys!"

Accompanied by the pair of seemingly identical dinosaurs, the man stopped before them. He was short and scruffy, easily fifty years old.

"You walk too fast," the dinosaur on the right groused. "Nicolai has to run."

"You walk too slow!" responded the one on the left. "He's young and healthy! Besides, you're clumsy! You almost stepped on him!"

"Gentlemen, please!" the human in the center cried.

"They speak too," Hugh whispered. "These blighters speak too!"

Both dinosaurs dipped their long necks and brought their heads close to examine Hugh. Nicolai had to leap back to get out of their way. The dinosaurs stopped inches before butting heads.

Hugh stared into the dark saucers of the dinosaurs' eyes. Their breath caused his hair to rustle slightly, as if it had been caught on a gentle breeze.

"Hello," he said, doing all he could to prevent his voice from cracking.

The dinosaurs angled their heads in unison, eyeing one another. As if they were one, the two dinosaurs said, "They speak *too!* These human blighters speak too!"

Hugh swallowed hard. "I don't suppose we could try this again, could we?"

Nicolai came forward, easing the heads of the great creatures from his path. "Don't mind them. They're both old, old, old and cranky!"

"We are not!" the dinosaurs protested.

The man touched the heads of each dinosaur, cradling one over each shoulder.

"All right, maybe a little," said the dinosaur on the right.

"Speak for yourself," said his companion.

Raymond stepped forward and shook the man's

hand. "Hello. Pleased to meet you. I'm Raymond Wilks."

"Hugh O'Donovan," his companion muttered. He could not take his gaze from the dinosaurs.

"Boo," one of them said.

Hugh flinched.

The man laughed. "I am Nicolai, seven mothers Russian. All this must seem strange to you. We will do our best to help you settle in to our ways. A moment."

Turning, Nicolai cried out. A dozen feet away, a young man with short red hair spun in his direction. Nicolai made an odd hand signal. The boy nodded and rushed off.

"What was that all about?" Hugh asked.

Nicolai grinned. "You're in luck. A messenger arrived a short time ago. I asked young Ryan to fetch her."

Bix said, "We need to send word to Waterfall City. Let them know to prepare for your arrival."

"I see," Hugh said warily. "And why will we be goin' there?"

"All newcomers spend time in Waterfall City," Bix said. "It is a place of learning."

Nicolai held up a hand. "There will be time for questions later," he said. "For now, you lads must be hungry. And you look as if you could use a change of clothes. Perhaps someplace quiet to lay your heads a while."

"I'd like to see more of this place," Raymond said,

his eyes widening as a pair of ostrich-like creatures bounded toward them. Both dinosaurs had red crests and made trilling noises.

Nicolai answered them in a strange singsong. Once the pair had vanished inside the mill, the burly man turned his gaze back to his guests.

"You spoke their language!" Raymond said.

"You'll find a knowledge of Saurian quite helpful," Nicolai said.

"Saurian?" Hugh asked.

Bix nudged him from behind. He turned and crouched beside her.

"I'm still not sure you're real or that any of this is happening," Hugh said.

"That's nice," Bix replied. "While you're deciding, scratch my crest? Itches!"

Hugh's hand trembled slightly as he touched Bix's crest. He scratched where she indicated, and Bix started to coo. The sound calmed the older boy.

"Saurian," Nicolai said, "can refer to any dinosaur, or the basic language shared by all."

"There are many offshoots," said one of the rose-colored dinosaurs behind Nicolai. "Each of our races has its own history and culture."

"Yes, yes!" his partner replied. "You fresh eggs ought to remember that."

"Fresh eggs?" Raymond asked.

"Newcomers," Hugh guessed. "Right?"

"Good!" Bix cried. "You're starting to understand

the way of things! Now, lower and to the left."

Hugh did as he was asked.

"Are there always so many people and so many dinosaurs here?" Raymond asked, jumping slightly as a creature taller than the windmill walked by. Raymond looked up but could see only the underside of the dinosaur's jaw!

"They could squash us and not even feel it!" Hugh cried.

"What do you think we are, barbarians?" one of the dinosaurs with Nicolai asked. "To think we would be so careless!"

Nicolai leaned in close. "We gave the twins here a surprise birthday party. How were we to know both of them loathe surprise birthday parties? Normally, they're in much better moods."

"I heard that," one of them growled. "It's because he gets all the presents!"

"And you eat everything in sight!"

Nicolai sighed. "They really do love each other. You'll have to take my word on that."

A door opened at the side of the mill, and a gaggle of small pink dinosaurs raced out. Not one of them was higher than the waists of the human children who ran after them.

Suddenly, a squall pierced the heavens. Raymond and Hugh looked up to see an odd creature flying over the mill. Its wings had a span of at least a half-dozen yards. They were bright yellow with pink and white highlights. The flying creature had a beak the length of a man. Its eyes were dark and probing.

On the flying creature's back was a young woman in a harness. She wore a blue costume with long white sleeves. Her hair was tucked within a helmet adorned by an azure crest.

The creature landed in a clearing off to their left. The rider came forward, removing her helmet. Her long red hair descended in waves. Behind her, the group of newly hatched dinosaurs trotted up to the winged creature. With curiosity and awe, the young dinosaurs stood staring up at their large, majestic visitor.

"The funny thing is," the young woman said, "you fellows have the same expression as the hatchlings over there. Have you never seen a Skybax before?"

Hugh looked at the messenger's kind features and admitted he had not.

"You must be newcomers. I'll give you this bit of advice. Keep your eyes and ears open."

"You mean there's danger here," Hugh said.

"No." She laughed and turned to Raymond. "*You* understand, don't you? I see it in your eyes."

"Not dangers," said Raymond. "Wonders!"

CHAPTER 5

To the east of the ivory shore where Raymond and Hugh first set foot on Dinotopia lay Waterfall City. For days the boys had been told stories of this wondrous place.

At last they had arrived. Hugh, Raymond, Bix, and their guide, a bronze-skinned man named Sompuchal, stood upon an outcropping of stone. The morning sun cast a golden glow upon the vast, shining city, which was perched above several waterfalls.

"That must be a bloomin' mirage," Hugh said. "It can't be real. It *can't*."

Sompuchal laughed at Hugh's comical expression. "Ah, but it *is*."

One of the only ways in or out of Waterfall City was by flying machines in the shape of Skybaxes. One of these airships now arced over their heads and came to a graceful landing near them. A half-dozen men were already gathered to assist in its launch.

The visitors were loaded into seats upon the seemingly rickety apparatus. Raymond leaned back in his wood chair atop the flying machine and delighted as the Wing Ambassador sent them on their journey. They sailed off the cliffside smoothly as Sompuchal waved good-bye. Hugh squeezed his eyes shut, denying himself the wonders Raymond took in with pleasure.

Waterfall City was breathtaking and masterfully designed. It borrowed from many cultures while still keeping an identity all its own. They flew over a pair of stone lion sentinels that might have been more at home in Egypt. Then they landed in the open courtyard of a building so grand it would put the British Parliament to shame.

"That wasn't so bad, was it?" Raymond asked.

Hugh's face was ashen. "If I ever have to do that again, *I*'ll be the one with the bleedin' nightmares!"

Hugh instantly regretted his words. Poor Raymond had woken up screaming practically every night since they had arrived on Dinotopia. The loss of his father still haunted him.

But Raymond didn't have time to care about Hugh's words. Hundreds of humans and Saurians suddenly flooded into the square to greet them. Raymond laughed and enjoyed every moment of the celebration. Hugh hid his misgivings beneath a practiced smile.

Musicians filled the streets, and acrobats tumbled this way and that. Everywhere the boys turned, some human or dinosaur was pressing close and issuing words of welcome and encouragement. They were introduced to so many people that before long the names and faces began to run together.

"You will be here for the next six months, learning our written language and history," Bix said as morning waned and the festivities came to a close.

"What about after that?" Hugh asked.

"That, my friends, greatly depends on the two of you. Don't worry, all will become clear in time. And remind me to tell you about your wonderful teacher!"

Before long they were ushered into one of the city's grand buildings. The quiet, empty Registry was a big change from the whirlwind of activity in the streets. They walked down a marble hall toward a long scroll fastened to a podium. A quill pen sat beside the parchment.

"Now, wait a minute," Hugh said, gazing at the scroll. "What's all this?"

"You are our guests," Bix said. "You are newcomers to our home and our ways. The Guest Registry is signed by all Dolphinbacks."

"Ah, so this is how it starts," Hugh said in a whisper to Raymond. "First we *register*, then they can start keepin' tabs on us, probably force us to work and gouge us with taxes!"

"Hugh," Raymond said, "do you ever think that maybe, just maybe, you're being silly?"

Hugh shrugged, then silently watched the younger

boy take up the quill and sign in, writing "physician's son" next to his name.

"Do me a favor?" Hugh asked, deciding to go along. "Sign in for me. By occupation, just put—*entrepreneur!*"

"Oh!" Raymond said with a touch of embarrassment. "Certainly, I'm sorry. It hadn't even occurred to me."

Hugh touched Raymond's wrist, stopping the boy before he could write Hugh's name.

"*What* hadn't occurred to ya?" Hugh asked pointedly.

"There's nothing to be ashamed of," Raymond said in a tone that was meant to be reassuring. "I've known lots of decent gents who weren't men of letters."

"Go on!" Hugh cried. "I can bloody well read and write."

"Then why ask me to sign in for you?"

Hugh's face flushed in embarrassment. He whispered, "I just wannit sure how to *spell* entrepreneur, that's all."

"Oh," Raymond said, swallowing hard. "To be honest—neither am I."

They looked at each other a moment, then burst out laughing. With a grin, Hugh took the quill from Raymond and signed the scroll. He took his best guess with the spelling.

After they left the Registry, Bix took the boys to their new quarters—a hostelry sponsored by the city for visitors. The huge five-storied building had marble columns and steepled archways. Its thick stone walls were adorned with strange symbols and beautiful drawings.

"What does that mean?" Raymond asked, pointing at a strange set of symbols:

Bix read the sign. "Home is within us all."

Hugh frowned. He didn't understand the saying, but he said nothing. The group climbed a long, spiraling stone staircase. They passed two landings. Even through the thick walls of the building, they could hear the rush of the city's many waterfalls.

On the fourth landing, they stopped. Bix nodded toward the door.

"Guess this one's ours," Hugh said, examining the door for some kind of knob. He pushed it open. "No lock, eh?"

Bix shook her head. "No need for one here."

"Would ya look a' this!" Hugh cried as he gazed at their spacious new quarters. Two beds were set up near the far gabled windows. A table sat in the middle of the single room, near a pair of chests and two tall wardrobes filled with clothing. A kitchen area was in the far corner.

"Well, I'll be," Hugh said. "We've got our own flat. And it's clean—if a bit damp."

Raymond nodded. Because of the many waterfalls and canals, a certain clamminess pervaded every inch of the city.

"Now, then," Hugh said. "What's this teacher business all about?"

"Oh, yes!" Bix lowered her voice and added, "Say nothing about his height. Most of his race grow much taller. He's quite sensitive about it."

"What I *meant* is, I don't remember bein' asked if I was interested in attendin' school."

Bix simply stared at him.

"Ah, well," Hugh finally said. "So this teacher, he's a real shorty, is he?"

An odd sound came from behind them. It resembled the noise a man might make clearing his throat, only it was deeper, more resounding, and clearly not made by a human. Turning sharply, the boys saw a dinosaur standing in the open doorway. The dinosaur entered the room, towering over the boys.

The creature walked on its hind legs and stood well over nine feet. It had pebbly skin and waves of garish color—bright greens and oranges laced with splotches of hot pink. A black and red silk robe adorned its body. But its most notable feature was its face, which had the unmistakable look of a duck.

"I suppose, from your expressions," the dinosaur

said dryly, "that you have never seen an Edmontosaurus before. In fact, I would guess that you boys haven't even bothered to learn that Bix here is a Protoceratops. No matter. All that will be seen to."

"Goody," Hugh said.

The Edmontosaurus went on. "We are duck-billed, as you can clearly tell, and have no front teeth. However, we are far from toothless."

The dinosaur opened its jaws wide, revealing hundreds of teeth wedged behind the front jaw. The dinosaur crossed its thin arms over its chest. It had three webbed fingers with neatly manicured nails. Its legs were thick, and its toes had two-inch nails that clicked impatiently on the ground. The dinosaur's tail moved about lazily behind it.

"Boys," Bix said, "this is your new teacher. His name is Sollis."

CHAPTER 6

"Pleased to meet you," Raymond said brightly to his new teacher.

"You really do look like a bleedin' duck," Hugh said.

"I believe we covered that," the Saurian said evenly. His crimson eyes remained fixed on Hugh. "So you don't believe in getting an education?"

Hugh raised his chin defiantly. He wondered if he would get a neck cramp from having to crane upward whenever addressing Sollis. "I know lots of blokes who told me they didn't learn nothin' in school that would help 'em survive on the streets. Just a waste o' time."

The Saurian angled his head slightly. "So you've never heard the phrase, '*Knowledge is power.*'"

"Sure, I have. It's like, if you're gonna run the old dodge on someone—y'know, a ruse, a trick—ya bloomin' well better know everythin' there is to know about him."

"So why don't you pretend you're out to...ah...

'run the old dodge' on *me*," Sollis said. "Make me believe you're a hardworking student out to better himself. Pretend you genuinely wish to learn what life on this island has to offer."

"Is that a challenge?" Hugh asked.

"I would say," the dinosaur replied.

"All right, Ducky," Hugh answered. "You've got yourself a deal."

The Saurian bowed slightly, then departed.

"Ducky?" Raymond asked.

Hugh grinned mischievously. "Just wanted to see if he'd let it get to him. But it looks like Sollis is made o' sterner stuff. I could get to like ol' Ducky, I really could."

Bix chirped up. "Come, my friends. I would like to show you more before nightfall."

They went downstairs and took to the glorious streets of Waterfall City. With all the activity surrounding them when they first arrived, the boys had not really been able to look around and appreciate the city's true magnificence.

The streets were alive with activity: dinosaurs pulling carts, people washing the flanks of the creatures, humans and dinosaurs engaged in conversation. Even here, close to the heart of the city, the crashing waterfalls sounded like thunder.

"Imagine it!" Raymond said, gazing at the splendor surrounding them. "Humans and Saurians working together as equals. More than that, people of every *race* living together, their quarrels made meaningless and justly forgotten."

"No need to imagine," Bix said in her trilling voice. "You have only to open your eyes."

They walked on down cobblestone streets. Grinning despite himself, Hugh shook his head. "This *is* a far cry from London," he said. "I'll not deny it. For one thing, the air's so crisp. There's no smell o' soot, no taint o' industry here. And the streets're so clean. Everythin' looks shiny and new, but it can't possibly *be* new. Building all this must've took decades. Centuries, even!"

"It is glorious," Raymond said.

Hugh turned to Bix. "Does everyone here have a home? A place to lay their heads at night?"

"Of course," Bix replied.

Hugh pursed his lips. "What of the workhouses?"

The dinosaur did not understand.

"You know, where they send people what can't pay their bills an' the like. The poor, the wretched? Like prisons!"

"There are no prisons," Bix said. "What need would we possibly have for those?"

Suddenly, a comfortingly familiar sight caught Hugh's attention. He bolted forward, leaving Raymond and Bix to chase after him. They caught up to him on the outer edge of a ring of children and Saurians who were playing some odd game of chance with colored stones. Hugh had pulled a teenager off to the side.

"So what do you have there, lad?" Hugh pointed at the pebbles in the boy's hand. "A day's wages? Show me the rules o' this game, 'n' I'll show you how to turn your winnings into enough cash to make ya fat for a week!"

The boy seemed uninterested, or perhaps just perplexed. The Saurian beside him, a Hadrosaurus with a wine-colored crest, nudged Hugh off with his tail.

Moments later, Hugh and the others were again walking down the cobbled street, following the course of the waters. They stopped to gaze at a spectacular archway that served as a bridge over the boat channel.

"I don't understand," Hugh said. "You tell us that people work in this place. All I wanted to do was help turn the game to his advantage. If I helped him make a profit, he would surely share it with his benefactor. Me!"

"Such schemes are fruitless here," Bix said. "People do what they must. In return, they are given what they need."

"I see," Raymond said. "You have a barter system. If I'm a gardener and I need a shed built, I go to a builder. I tell him I'll plant him a garden if he'll build me a shed. To get what we want, we trade!"

"You mean there's no *money* on this island?" Hugh cried.

"We did away with such things long ago," said Bix.

"Then what are those colored stones for?" Hugh asked indignantly.

Raymond cleared his throat. "I think they're like marbles. They're not really worth anything."

"You expect me to believe Dinotopians play games of chance simply for their amusement?" Hugh asked. "And there is no such thing as money on this island? Then how do you take the measure of a man's worth?"

"By his deeds," said Bix.

Suddenly, a chilling cry over their heads made both boys jump. A shadow fell over them, and they heard the flapping of leathery wings. A breeze blew by them, and a creature with a wingspan of more than a half-dozen yards whipped past. A Skybax!

The creature had the long neck of a swan, but its head was much more imposing. Its eyes burned with a dark intelligence. Its body was reptilian, with an almond-shaped torso and two long rubbery legs capped with claws.

Raymond thought it was a graceful, majestic creature the color of an autumn twilight, amber-stained with pastel shades of blue and green. But there was something wrong with its wings. They seemed frayed and scarred, as if they had been badly burned once. The creature had to correct its flight twice before it alighted on its target, a small sailboat.

The pair of humans aboard the craft leaped into the channel's waters. The Skybax ripped through the boat's sail with its rapier-like fingers and used its strong wings to slap at the jutting column of the mainsail. The boat was capsized with a single blow.

"Well, now!" Hugh said. "Look at that! It seems not *everyone* here is so bleedin' happy! I knew there'd be malcontents. I wonder what was done to him to make him so angry!"

Bix made a low, unhappy sound. In a sharp voice, seething with impatience, she said, "Windchaser's reasons are his own. We understand why he has lost his way. Do not *judge* what you do not *understand*."

Hugh was speechless. He bit his lip and watched with the others as the Skybax teetered and nearly plunged into the waters. It looked like a child's toy, a kite flailing at the end of a tether. Then it righted itself and headed toward another of the ships in the waterway. A half-dozen humans and two Saurians leaped overboard.

The Skybax let out a triumphant wail and changed course an instant before it would have crashed through the larger ship's sail. Circling above the area for a moment, the Skybax loosed a squall that might have been a laugh or a cry of pain.

Raymond could not look away from this creature. He did not have to see the sadness in Bix's eyes as the Protoceratops regarded the Skybax. Raymond's heart knew at once that this creature was in pain. The part of him that had trained at his father's side as a healer responded to that pain, while another part of him felt an eerie kinship to the Skybax.

Circling once more, the Skybax headed right for Raymond and the others. Hugh dove to the ground.

Raymond did not move, certain the Skybax would not harm him.

Careening to a halt, the tip of its beak only a few feet from Raymond, the Skybax touched down lightly on its hind legs. Flapping its mighty wings for balance, the creature kicked up a terrible wind. Raymond held his ground, his hand slowly reaching up.

For a moment, Raymond's gaze locked with the Skybax's. The boy's hand lightly grazed its beak. He saw something in the creature's eyes, a pain he had seen reflected in the mirror every day since he had lost his father. There was a darkness in the Skybax's eyes. It seemed almost as deep as the nightmarish abyss in which Raymond lost himself every night as he dreamed about the tragic events on the *Redemption*.

Raymond sank to one knee and fished his father's pocketwatch from his boot. He stood, ignoring any danger, and held it out for the Skybax to see.

With another ear-piercing squall, the Skybax reared back, flapping its wings frantically. Raymond could not tell if the creature was angered or frightened. All he knew was that his gesture, which even he did not fully understand, had been rejected.

The Skybax turned and glided off, leaving Raymond to watch after it with a haunting sense of longing.

CHAPTER 7

Sollis arrived at the boys' quarters the next morning. It was a sunny day. Raymond was at the window searching the clear skies for any glimpse of the wounded Skybax. But the majestic creature did not appear.

Hugh sat on his bed, leaning against the headboard. His arms were crossed over his chest, and a wicked smile played across his handsome face. "Come on, Ducky. Surprise and delight me."

The Edmontosaurus laughed, enjoying the challenge Hugh presented. "First, I have an announcement. Bix was called away on an urgent matter. She will return as soon as she can."

He asked the boys to sit at the table in the middle of the room. There he set down several scrolls. One was a map of Dinotopia.

"The island was once connected to a major land mass," Sollis said, pointing to where the break had occurred. "When perpetually dark skies and freezing temperatures threatened to wipe out the many species of dinosaur, the Saurians took refuge in the cavernous underground referred to as the World Beneath. They emerged when it was safe. For tens of millions of years they have evolved into sentient and wise creatures."

"Some of whom look like ducks," Hugh said.

"The fortunate ones," Sollis replied.

Raymond smiled. He noticed that Hugh did not use Sollis's height as a means to taunt him.

"We will be studying all manner of dinosaur over the coming months," Sollis said. "Today, I will tell you more about the island's geography. One must first consider that Dinotopia is completely cut off from the outside world. This island is surrounded by an impassable coral reef. A system of tides and winds prevents navigation, making it impossible to leave the island by boat or even by balloon, as was suggested by a recent Dolphinback."

"Ya mean we can't *ever* leave this place?" Hugh asked, stunned.

"No egg rolls from the nest," Sollis said. "This was not explained to you?"

"No," Hugh said. He looked as if his future had just been snatched from his hands.

Raymond shook his head, equally startled. "I assumed the choice was ours."

"I am sorry to be the one to tell you," Sollis said. "Though I would ask you to consider this: you have been with us for many days. If the thought of returning to the outside world did not occur to you, it may be because you have no desire to do so."

"I dunno about *that*," Hugh said quickly.

Later, after their first day of lessons was finished and Sollis had departed, Hugh turned to Raymond. "I won't believe I'm a prisoner. They just want us to think there's no way to escape. The Dinotopians have a nice little setup here. They like fresh blood now and then to keep things goin'. It also lets 'em find out what's goin' on in the outside world. But no way to get out? I don't believe that for a minute."

Raymond was saddened by his friend's words. "Has anyone here lied to you?"

Hugh shrugged. "How'd I know?"

Raymond ignored his friend's sarcastic reply. "Saying we're *trapped* is only one way to look at the situation. Think of what Dinotopia has to offer. All that's wrong with the outside world is kept from us here. War was done away with centuries ago. There is food for all. People are content."

"So *you* say," Hugh replied. "You're believin' all this. Me, I was schooled on the streets. My teachers told me, 'You never get somethin' for nothin'. If someone has a gift in one hand, they got a dagger in the other.'"

"There's not much I can say to that," Raymond said.

"Didn't think there would be. I'm just lettin' you know: you do whatever you want with your back. I'm watching mine."

*　　*　　*

Several weeks passed. Raymond applied himself to his studies with great vigor. It seemed the more information he crammed into his head, the less severe his nightmares were when he went to sleep. Yet he could not get rid of them completely. The loss of his father from his life was still fresh and hard to bear.

When Raymond felt saddest, he would turn his attention to the sky and look again for the wounded Skybax. He could not forget it. Often, he'd make sketches of the great winged creature during lectures. Soon he was overwhelming his teacher with questions about the Skybax's many mysteries. Sollis commended his student on his dedication to learning.

In contrast, Hugh barely paid attention during Sollis's teachings. Several weeks passed before the Saurian came to understand the kind of motivation Hugh needed.

The morning was very dreary. Raymond was unable to keep himself from yawning. Hugh stared at a particular spot on the wall of their quarters with an unfocused gaze. Rain fell outside their window.

Sollis unraveled a scroll and cleared his throat. *"Boredom is a worthless currency. Why is it then the price we often pay to get what we want?"*

"If I knew that, I wouldn't be sitting here, would I?" Hugh asked.

"Ah," Sollis said, encouraged. "You approve of the sentiment?"

Hugh shrugged. "Sounds like whoever said it was

a plain talker. I always approve of *that*."

"You're bored, aren't you?"

"Oh, no, Ducky." Hugh yawned. "I wouldn't say that."

"Of course not. It would be impolite. And at your heart, you are a diplomat."

"A diplomat, eh?" asked Hugh, surprised.

"The words I read to you are from Laegreffon, a popular philosopher and diplomat. Do you understand what he's getting at?"

"O' course I do," Hugh said. "To get what we want, we sometimes have to do things we don't like. We have to be patient."

"Tell me. When you were in London, what did you do?" asked Sollis.

"Besides stealin'?" Hugh let out a ragged breath. "I don't know if you'd understand."

"Try me."

"Well, in London, everythin' was different. There ya was a fool to play by the rules. Ya could work till ya dropped, and it hardly made a difference.

"See, me dad was a cheap-jack, hawkin' chains and carvin' knives at the fair. Me ma was a crossing sweeper. Five or six shillings a week for riskin' her neck. I can still see her, dodging in and out o' traffic, sweepin' the filth from the street so the rich wouldn't get it on their nice shoes.

"Me dad died before he was thirty, and me ma was struck by a carriage. I had me share of the workin' man's life, too. I was a mudlark, goin' into the Thames when it was at low tide, prayin' I wouldn't cut me feet on glass. I searched in the muck for coal, rope, bones, and copper nails. That's when I was ten. Before that, I was used as a climbin' boy."

The Edmontosaurus nodded gravely. "Why then would you wish to return there?"

"'Cause there ya knew what was what. There weren't no secrets. No one holdin' out false hope."

"I see," said the teacher. "You do understand that there are no secrets here, either. And as far as hope goes, Laegreffon said it best. *Hope can be a fool's game, or the salvation of us all. Your choice.*'"

"Right then," Hugh said. "So tell me this. What happens to me at the end o' the six months if I don't get a shinin' letter o' approval from ya? What's the penalty?"

"There's no penalty except what you bring on yourself," Sollis said. "You have great potential that you are gleefully wasting. *Life is opportunity. Why settle when there is so much out there?*'"

Hugh's gaze narrowed. "So ya say there's no secrets in this place. Just knowledge I haven't got yet."

The Edmontosaurus nodded.

"All right," Hugh said. "Prove it."

Sollis took the boys to Waterfall City's magnificent library. The building was filled with endless corridors and murals. The walls of the reading rooms were three stories high and lined with scrolls. Many visitors were looking through the titles. All that marred the library's perfection was Waterfall City's usual dampness.

Hugh looked bored as Raymond raced about, translating what titles he could. Hugh barely listened until he heard Raymond call out, "The Secret for Transmuting Base Metal into Gold."

"Wot's that, ya say?" Hugh said, whirling.

Raymond took down the scroll and handed it to his friend. Hugh opened it with trembling fingers. His mind whirled with the possibilities. If he knew the secret for turning base metal into gold, he could become wealthy beyond imagining. He turned to his teacher, who was following close behind.

"This is some kind o' bloomin' joke, now innit?" Hugh asked.

"No," Sollis said. "Someone took the trouble to write it down, didn't he?"

Hugh growled in frustration as he saw the scroll was littered with characters and formulae he could not read. "Raymond! Quickly. What does it say?"

Raymond was about to respond when Sollis stopped him.

"No," Sollis said. "Hugh, if you want the secret so badly, you can learn to read it for yourself. What you have in your hands is a copy. There are others on the shelf. Borrow this one and see if you can unravel its mysteries."

Hugh frowned. He spent the rest of the day doing

his best to come up with a way to entice Raymond into helping him. But the younger boy refused.

The next day, Hugh plopped down in his chair and was all smiles as Sollis arrived to begin his teachings. "Ah, well. Never let it be said I wasn't dragged in kickin' and screamin'. All right, governor. Educate me. I bleedin' dare ya!"

CHAPTER 8

Sollis had a feeling that something wonderful would occur today. A month had gone by since Hugh began to apply himself to his studies. During that time, the boy made several attempts at translating the secret for turning base metal into gold. On his last try, Hugh was *so* close. Sollis told him as much. Hugh did not become cross or frustrated. Instead, he applied himself that much harder.

"All right," Hugh said nervously as their lessons began. "I think I got it."

"Then read the scroll," Sollis said.

Hugh did as he was commanded. When he was finished, he looked up anxiously.

Sollis was grinning. "Perfection!"

Hugh shouted in delight and hurled the scroll into the air. Laughing, he leaned so far back in his chair that he fell down. Raymond moved to help, and Hugh dragged the boy down with him. Hugh grabbed him in a bear hug. Raymond struggled playfully to extricate himself.

"You're crazy!" Raymond cried.

"It's true!" Hugh said. "Bloomin' starkers!"

Sollis laughed. "My friends, I believe both of you have earned a well-deserved day off. Take it with my compliments."

Hugh reached out and messed up Raymond's hair. "Let's go!"

The boys took to the streets, and Hugh cried, "It's a glorious day, Raymond!"

Following behind, Raymond had to agree. The sky was clear blue—not one cloud. A soft breeze drifted over the streets from the canal waters.

"Hey!" Hugh said, turning and placing his hands on Raymond's shoulders. "Want to have some fun?"

"Sure!" Raymond said. "Like what?"

Hugh laughed. "Watch closely."

The older boy began to eye the passersby like a natural predator, though his expression seemed innocent.

Suddenly, Hugh was jostled by an older man who laughed, then begged pardon. Hugh patted the man's tunic and said nothing was amiss. After they'd proceeded another block, a mischievous glint lit Hugh's eyes.

"Tell me you didn't," Raymond said.

"As you will," Hugh said as he revealed a pocket-sized timepiece in his palm. "I didn't."

Raymond snatched the timepiece and ran back in the direction of the older man. He caught up to the man and returned it. Raymond fumbled a bit as he explained that the item had fallen and that he and Hugh found it. The man thanked him.

Moments later, Raymond saw Hugh on the steps of the city's great library. Hugh held out two similar timepieces, a bracelet, and a ring. Raymond sighed, wondering what was to become of his friend.

He sat down on the steps. "Why are you still doing this? There's no reason for you to steal."

"No reason?" Hugh asked. He leaned in close. "There's *every* reason. I have to keep sharp. True, I translated the scroll. I understand its words. But I'm no metalworker. Nor am I a chemist. Once I'm back home, I'll have to hire people to do the actual work of makin' lead into gold. I'll need money for that." He rattled the stolen belongings. "This is how I'll get it."

"Hugh—"

"Don't say it. I know Sollis claims there's no way to leave Dinotopia. But I've heard there's a map room somewhere on the island. It's bound to have a course charted through the reef."

Raymond considered mentioning the breakers and the deadly winds, but he knew his words would not stop his friend.

A noise came from behind the boys. They were blocking the exit of a green-skinned Triceratops. Hugh led Raymond away from the library steps.

Soon they were leaning against a fountain. A

dozen feet away, an apprentice to a Dragonhorn player was performing a sidewalk concerto.

"I want you to come with me," Hugh said. "We'll go into business together. We'll be rich. What do you say?"

Raymond squeezed his eyes shut. From overhead he heard the caw of a Skybax, and his eyes opened at once. But it was not the wounded Skybax—the one he was still hoping to see again.

"Come on," Hugh said. "Haven't you ever done anything the remotest bit exciting? Have you no fire in your spirit?"

"I suppose…I'll have to think about it," Raymond said distantly.

Hugh nodded, not paying any attention to his friend's serious expression. "Sure, sure. Take your time. Just remember what Laegreffon says: *'No experience is wasted.'* I've made mistakes, but I've learned from them. *'Every action has its purpose.'* I can hardly believe it, Raymond. Finally, I'm going to *be* someone!"

"You already *are* someone. Don't you understand that?"

"Come on, don't be a stupid git. Either this is all an act or these people are bloomin' pitiful."

"What do you mean?" Raymond asked.

"The Dinotopians," said Hugh. "They can't be so bloomin' good. I mean, if I was to believe that, I'd have to believe some of the other stuff they said, like there bein' no way out o' this place. Then where would I be?"

"Right where you're going to be anyway, Hugh. They're not lying to you. All they're trying to do is help you find what's inside you. Help you to learn about this place and be happy."

Hugh was still not listening. "You know the best part?" Hugh asked. "I've been takin' stuff for weeks. Found a little hidey hole to stash it all in. Ain't no one here's got the first clue it was me that's been takin' their things."

"You're wrong," Raymond said.

Hugh stared at him. He kept silent while a procession went past, several dinosaurs and a gaggle of humans. Hugh's joyous mood was finally fading. He waited until they were alone again, then he snarled, "What are you *talkin'* about?"

"They've known all along it was you doing the robberies."

"Ridiculous! I been slicker than ever."

"That's not the point. These people don't steal. It's not in their nature. They knew it had to be you doing the stealing because there's no one else who knows how. What they don't know is *why*. In any case, they decided it would be best to let you get it out of your system."

Hugh's dark eyes narrowed. "You're just tryin' to get me to mess up, aren't ya? Ya want me to make a mistake and get caught!"

"No. I'm your friend," Raymond said. "I'm trying to help you see what you're doing to yourself."

"Ya think ya know everythin', don't ya? Just like all these people. Well, how 'bout we make a little wager? If you're right, if they know all 'bout what I've been doin', I'll *burn* the scroll. I'll learn just for the sake of learnin'. I'll try to fit in. How'd that be?"

"Don't do *me* any favors," Raymond replied. "Do it for yourself."

Hugh smiled. "Is it a bet?"

"All right. Sure," Raymond said, giving up.

"Don't ya want to know what you'll have to do when ya lose?" Hugh asked as he turned to go.

"I won't lose," Raymond said unhappily. "I'm sorry, Hugh."

"You're gonna be in for a rude surprise," Hugh warned playfully as he jaunted off.

"One of us will be."

Over the coming hours, Hugh decided to test Raymond's claim that the people of Dinotopia were turning a blind eye toward his petty thieving. Hugh walked into the shop of a metalworker and picked up a beautifully adorned bracelet. "I'm takin' this. Got any problem wi' me *stealin'* it?"

"No, young sir. You must need it more than I."

Whirling in confusion, Hugh put the bracelet in his oversized pouch and left.

Next, he went to the library, took several original

scrolls, and waved them before the wizened librarian's nose. The old man smiled benevolently and said, "If your need is so strong, so be it."

"What if I just threw them on a fire?"

"Then knowledge would be lost."

Grunting in frustration, Hugh stormed off. The rest of the day, he met with the same reactions! No one tried to stop him from taking what he wanted, though he clearly had no use for the things he stole and he never offered any service as payment.

Finally, as twilight approached, Hugh found a six-year-old girl playing alone near a gabled dwelling. By now his large pouch was stuffed full of goods. The girl had soft auburn hair and a joyous laugh. Clutched in her hand was a doll that she clearly loved. She spoke to it, played with it, and hugged it close.

Hugh snatched the doll away and waited. He knew it would only be a moment before the child started to wail. Her cries would bring someone to give him a merry chase. Instead, she looked at him with profound hurt in her eyes. His own shame caused him to give the toy back.

"Hello," a deep, throaty voice called from the porch behind Hugh. He spun and saw a woman with reddish hair, soft gray eyes, and a kind, forgiving smile.

The woman said, "I'm Dominique's stepmother, Moira. Four mothers Irish."

"You're not the child's mother?" Hugh asked.

"There was a terrible accident," the woman explained. "Dominique's mother was taken from us. That doll is all the child has as a remembrance."

"You saw me take the doll?" Hugh asked.

"I did."

"And you would have let me have it?"

"If you needed it that badly. If it meant that much to you."

Hugh recoiled as if he had been struck. "Don't any of you people understand? To my way of thinkin', there's only gettin' away with somethin' or bein' punished for failin' to cover your tracks."

"Perhaps you need a new way of thinking." The woman sighed. "I've heard you have a good heart and a keen eye for seeing around corners. That's quite a gift."

"I dunno," Hugh said, confused. A part of him wanted the woman to scold him, to tell him he was a worthless wretch, but she did not.

She smiled. "There must be a goodness just waiting to blossom within you. If not, you wouldn't have protected the boy on the ship, and the dolphins wouldn't have saved *both* your lives. Would you like to come in and talk for a time? My friend Allyshar, an Ornithomimus, is cooking a fine broth. I'm sure you can smell it. Will you?"

Hugh was torn. Even Dominique, the gentle child, welcomed him to stay.

Offering an apology, Hugh hefted his sack and left

the gabled dwelling. On the way home, he returned much of what he had stolen and vowed to spend the next day giving back the rest.

He could no longer deny the facts. The goodwill of the Dinotopians was *not* a trick. Suddenly he understood. Their society had a nobility and strength worth more than any physical object.

Nevertheless, this knowledge did not cheer Hugh. If anything, it made him feel worse. He wasn't worthy to live among these people.

Hugh entered the room he shared with Raymond quite late. He fumbled around in the darkness until he could light a lamp. Then he dumped the scroll into a metal bucket and started a small fire inside it.

Raymond woke to see Hugh staring silently down at the flames. In the dim light, Raymond blinked in surprise. He would swear he saw his friend brush quickly at a wet droplet that had slipped down his cheek. No words were said.

Soon both lads were asleep. But several hours later, in the middle of the night, Hugh woke from a nightmare. In the dream, he was back in London, realizing he would never amount to anything.

Moving quietly, Hugh went to the worktable. He lit a single candle, took out a sheet of parchment, and recopied the formula for gold from memory. Then he hid the new parchment in his boot and blew out the candle.

He slept the rest of the night without dreams.

"Happy birthday, Raymond!" called a chorus of voices.

The newly turned fourteen-year-old smiled at his friends. He had not expected a party. Sollis had asked Raymond to look up a scroll at the library. When he returned, dozens of humans and Saurians were waiting in his quarters. Even Bix was there!

Raymond wished that his father could have lived to see this day. The elder Wilks would have loved Dinotopia. Raymond looked over at the only other survivor of the prison ship *Redemption*.

Hugh O'Donovan was somewhat changed since the night he lost his wager with Raymond. He studied without complaining. He was gracious and kind, and he did what was expected of him. His speech and grammar even improved, becoming a shade more proper.

But the fire that had been in Hugh's eyes was now dimmed. Raymond knew why. Hugh still didn't believe that he belonged on Dinotopia.

The party was a great success. The guests ate and played games. Raymond received many presents, but it was not until the festivities were over that he was given the gift that meant the most to him.

Only Bix, Sollis, and Hugh remained with Raymond. Bix said, "Because of your overwhelming progress in your studies and the great interest you have expressed in the Skybaxes, Sollis and I have arranged for you to visit Skybax Camp for three weeks. There you will be given basic instruction in the way of the Skybax and will even be taken on a short ride by a seasoned Skybax."

Raymond was overwhelmed. Though his solitary and brief encounter with the wounded Skybax was now firmly in the past, the memory of that event still burned inside of him. He was fascinated by the winged creatures and could think of no greater delight than spending time learning how to ride one of them.

"Father and I went on a balloon ride once," Raymond said, the words tumbling forth. "I'd love to go!"

Raymond's upbeat mood faded somewhat when Bix did not make the same offer to Hugh.

"It's all right," Hugh said, the glimmer of expectation leaving his dark eyes. "You know the sight of those winged blighters turns me into a bleedin' git! You go. I'll be fine."

Raymond shook his head and put his hand on Bix's flank. "I'm not going without Hugh."

"Hugh may accompany you, but he is too old to be trained as a Skybax Rider."

"I'll sweep out the dung," Hugh said with a passion that surprised everyone. "Take care of the stables or whatever they have."

"Hmmmm," Sollis said. "What you describe is a time-honored and special task. Many great responsibilities go along with such an undertaking."

"I know I haven't done much to deserve the faith

you've shown in me," Hugh said, "but I'd like to be with my friend. I'll work hard. You know I will!"

"Then come you may," Bix said. "This might be exactly what both of you need!"

Hugh smiled. "As Laegreffon might have said, *Words of gratitude fail me. Better to make you proud with my deeds.*'"

Sollis beamed at Hugh. "I know how hard it's been. I'm so proud of all you've achieved."

Hugh hesitated as unexpected feelings overwhelmed him. For the first time in his life, someone was actually proud of him.

"By the heavens," Raymond said. "I think you've left him speechless!"

Later that night, after Raymond had gone to sleep, Hugh stared at the formula for gold he had recopied.

He walked slowly across the room to a blazing candle. A basin was close by. All he had to do was set the parchment on fire and forget about it. Then he could get on with his life.

He picked up the candle, then stopped. He could not do it! Instead, with a ragged sigh, he leaned in and blew out the flame.

CHAPTER 9

On the day Raymond and Hugh arrived at Skybax Camp, they took in the sights and sounds of a colorful celebration. The camp was indeed the marvel Raymond had imagined, even though it was located far from Canyon City.

Canyon City was the island's center of all Skybax Rider training. Raymond had been told of its amazing vistas. It was said to be carved out of the stone canyon walls, and its people lived among the clouds.

Here at Skybax Camp, riders did not fly from high stone ledges. Instead, they leaped from carefully crafted man- and dinosaur-made platforms. Some of these high, brilliantly colored platforms were even built to look like various dinosaurs.

The sky above the camp was clear and blue. It was easy to spot the half-dozen Skybaxes circling and performing tricks with their riders.

Raymond took in his new surroundings with excited interest. The camp was divided into three color-coded training areas and a central fairgrounds, where Raymond and Hugh had been all morning.

Each week new inductees were welcomed to the red, or novice, area with a splendid celebration. The Dinotopians prided themselves on their finely developed sense of pageantry. Even the students who had progressed into the yellow and blue areas and had seen this same celebration two and three times were looking up at the sky in delight.

Above Raymond now were two Skybax Riders involved in a friendly contest known as Air Jousting. Two lightly armored opponents went after each other like ancient knights. The spears they used for jousting were actually long sticks with heavy padding on one end. They called them thump-dumpers.

The crowd cheered as the warriors made another run. This time, one of the riders was dismounted. The crowd gasped as the rider plummeted to earth! Then his parachute opened and the rider's sharp descent slowed.

The fairgrounds looked to Raymond like a life-size kaleidoscope! Everywhere Raymond looked, he saw a mad joyous swirl of bright activities: the four-tiered tent awnings, the brilliant costumes of inductees and riders, and the naturally dazzling colorings of the many dinosaurs visiting the camp.

Diving just over the heads of the crowd was a pair of Skybaxes and riders made up like court jesters. Raymond and Hugh laughed when one came close enough to knock the hat from the head of a man standing near them. Next came a stunning air ballet by two more Skybaxes and riders. A small band on the ground provided the sprightly music.

Before it was finished, Raymond felt hands on him. He was too relaxed to be startled or to offer much resistance as he found himself hoisted up to ride one of the long-neck dinosaurs attending the celebration.

"Hugh!" Raymond cried, gesturing for his friend to join him.

"Not for me, I'm afraid," Hugh said with a laugh. The older boy's gaze drifted to the golden ridges of mountains in the far distance. Something was coming from that direction—another Skybax. Odd. He had been told there would be only six Skybaxes present, no more. Apparently, this was a surprise guest.

As the Skybax flew closer, Hugh felt his heart sink. He recognized the creature quickly coming toward the crowd, and he tried to shout a warning. But few paid any attention.

The incoming Skybax forced an ear-piercing cry to rip from its throat. The sound tore through the noise of the celebration, and heads turned to see what was happening.

It was the same burned and wounded Skybax who had attacked the ships in the harbor at Waterfall City. He seemed to be flying in now for a repeat performance here!

The wounded Skybax careened toward another

Skybax and rider, sweeping the rider off with its wing. The woman dropped a dozen feet onto a soft patch of earth and quickly rebounded.

With a terrible screech, the rampaging Skybax ripped through a tent awning. It then dropped even lower to slice a wide path through the frightened crowd. There was no question in anyone's mind: this was *not* part of the celebration! The wounded Skybax seemed quite crazed, and people began to flee the area.

Still riding astride the long-neck dinosaur, Raymond turned and saw the wounded Skybax. The creature flew straight at him, but Raymond did not feel the slightest fear. Their gazes locked, and suddenly the wounded Skybax veered off. He climbed higher and higher, gaining speed and altitude until finally he became a mere speck in the vast blue sky.

At the edge of the crowd, Hugh was no longer staring at the Skybax. His gaze was fixed on his friend.

Raymond's expression was tense with a strange kind of longing. Hugh could see that this creature was somehow important to Raymond—maybe more important than Hugh.

The thought was unsettling for Hugh. *Very* unsettling, at that.

The next day Raymond began his training. He was unaccustomed to the harsh physical demands at Skybax Camp, but he quickly adjusted.

He'd already spent months trying to forget the trauma on the *Redemption* by immersing himself in his studies. Now he was grateful for the relief and release he found through pure physical exercise.

His instructor, Hikaro, who was five mothers Japanese, urged his students to find something within themselves he called *Heiki*, or tranquillity. The best way to do that, he said, was by putting the body to work when the mind was tired or troubled.

Many of the students found the notion absurd, but they quickly came to realize their instructor knew best. That night, Raymond slept better than he had since he and his father left England. There were no nightmares, only a gentle dream of flying.

On the second day, Raymond felt ready to learn more about the ways of the Skybax Rider.

"*Tszri-Ai*," Hikaro said. "That means balance. Balance is everything."

Today the instructor was accompanied by two Saurians. The two wore emblems on their costumes—a Skybax in silhouette with a single raised wing—to denote their rank as assistants to the instructor. They led the children to a room containing a large, long board and several practice mats.

Hikaro ordered his students to watch as he lay facedown on the board. The dinosaurs gripped either side of the board and lifted Hikaro into the air. They jostled him, doing their best to overturn him or force him to slide off.

The lithe, black-haired man remained on the board without ever using his hands to grip the edges. Finally, Hikaro drew his feet up under his body and balanced only on his knees while the dinosaurs violently shook the board and did their best to uproot him.

When the display was over, Hikaro stood and pointed at Raymond. "Your turn!"

Raymond's heart thundered as he lay down on the board. The assistants lifted him up, but they were easy on him. He lasted fifteen seconds before he slid. Instead of gripping with his hands, Raymond allowed himself to fall. Hikaro complimented him.

Once the other students had their turn, they were all led to another room. This one contained an odd contraption that looked like a wooden shower. It was enclosed on three sides with a complex rigging hanging above. A harness dangled from the strange roof. Pulleys and levers were visible on the sides.

This time, another student was chosen to go first. Raymond watched as the other boy was secured in the harness.

"Again, as on the board," Hikaro told the students, "you may not use your hands to grip." Hikaro smiled. "All must be achieved through the distribution of your weight."

The Saurians went to work on the controls at the side of the booth. Suddenly the floor began to rise and tip beneath the lad in the harness, hurling him this way and that. Within a few seconds he was gripping the harness, trying to fight off dizziness. Hikaro expressed mild disappointment, then welcomed the next student.

When the long day was over, Raymond was allowed a bath before returning to his dormitory. Bix caught up with him before he could reach the red building.

Night was approaching, and the sky was streaked with amber, blue, and green. *The same colors as the wounded Skybax*, thought Raymond.

He turned to Bix and said, "I want to ask you about that Skybax. The one that tried to ruin the celebration two days ago...the same one we saw in Waterfall City—"

"A sad creature," Bix said.

"Why does he behave like that? What's wrong with him?"

Bix sighed. "His name is Windchaser. He and his rider were once highly regarded on Dinotopia. They found a child who had run off and become lost, a child that might have died if not for them. Later, they were messengers, always dependable. Later still, they showed their valor by risking their lives again and again to save others."

"What happened?"

"There was a fire. Windchaser's rider—his name was Daniel—was trapped in a burning building. Windchaser tried to rescue Daniel, but there was no hope."

"So that's how his wings were burned," Raymond said, "and why he doesn't fly so well all the time."

"Yes, but he might have recovered from his injuries had he received treatment in time. There are special Dinotopian herbs and salves that would have lessened the damage done by the burns. He refused to allow anyone near him."

"Why?" Raymond asked, his worry mounting. "I mean, I know a Skybax and his rider are close, but someone else could have ridden him—"

"The bond between a Skybax and his rider is the commitment of a lifetime. Windchaser blames himself for Daniel's death, or so we all believe. He will allow no other rider to approach him."

"So, he's been acting this way for some time."

"Oh, yes! The Skybax is depressed over his fate. He often becomes quite surly."

"What else does he do?"

Bix sighed. "Windchaser interrupts training sessions with other Skybaxes and their riders. He makes mischief. Sometimes he seems to get pleasure only from making others miserable. Even if he regained full flight, no rider would ever trust him."

No rider but me, Raymond thought. "Tell me. If I wanted to find Windchaser, where would I go?"

Bix hesitated, then told him.

That evening, Hugh threw himself down in a huff upon the bunk next to Raymond's.

"What's wrong?" asked Raymond.

"Oh, nothing *really,*" Hugh groused. "It's just that nothing is simple to these people. There's a ceremony for this, a ritual for that, a time and place for everything. You don't want to know what goes into actually bathing a Skybax. I mean, you have to sing a song, like some rotter on the stage. Amazin', I tell you. The worst thing is, I'm starting to *like* it!"

Raymond tried not to smile too broadly as Hugh went on to recite the many tasks he performed today. Despite all of Hugh's complaining, there was a true respect for the customs he described. Raymond took this as a sure sign that, at last, Dinotopia might be working its magic on his friend.

Long after Hugh fell off to sleep, Raymond found himself again thinking about the wounded Skybax. He considered the dreams that had been visited upon him recently, visions of flying free among the clouds.

Suddenly, he knew what he had to do.

CHAPTER 10

Raymond *had* to see Windchaser, and that meant sneaking away from camp.

Raymond waited until the end of his first week of training. A day of rest had been earned, and Raymond knew he could get away without being noticed.

Bix had already told him the location of Windchaser's lair. The craggy rise was a good distance away. Traveling on foot was definitely out. Not only would it take longer than a day to get there and back, but Raymond's escape could be tracked. A Skybax out for a morning flight would spot him easily.

Raymond decided to stow away in a supply wagon departing at dawn. He had learned the wagon's route a day earlier and knew it would take him close enough to the mountains in the east.

He hid in the wagon and tried to remain as quiet as possible. After a few hours of bumps and jostles, Raymond peeked out from beneath the canvas curtain covering the wagon's cargo. He was almost there!

When the wagon finally made the turn bringing it closest to the mountains, Raymond clutched the small bag he had loaded with supplies. After taking a deep breath, he jumped from the wagon and rolled, forcing his body to relax and absorb the jarring impact.

When he finished his rolling, he sat up, dusted himself off, and surveyed the foothills of the mountains. They looked to him like two opposing stone giants. But Raymond remained determined as ever as he rose to his feet. Slinging his bag over his shoulder, he began his long hike.

After a time, he approached a narrow pass between the craggy sentinels. The walkway was covered in shadow and very dark, despite the afternoon sun. It took Raymond longer than he would have liked to navigate its treacherous length.

Several times he put his foot forward and found it resting on nothing but empty air. There were drops he feared might have deposited him into the World Beneath—or at least into a pit from which there would be no escape.

Turning a corner, he finally saw a patch of brilliance. He quickly emerged onto a stone lip overlooking a churning canal. Raymond had learned that Dinotopians often took canoe rides along this canal. With any luck, a canoe would be left on his side of the channel.

Luck, it seemed, was with him today. Raymond took the canoe out.

At first, he was relieved to be floating carefree on the cool, choppy waters. Then suddenly, as if in response to Raymond's challenge, something leaped from the fast current—a large black stone, the size of Bix!

When Raymond looked again, he realized his mistake. The stone had not moved; it had simply come into view unexpectedly as the canoe dropped from a crest and slammed down toward the stationary rock.

With a cry, Raymond leaped overboard an instant before the canoe could strike the rock. The water was ice-cold, and he immediately felt for some anchor so that he would not be swept downstream. His hands found a twisted branch as the lightened canoe slid past the slick surface of the stone, missing it by a matter of inches.

Letting go of the branch, Raymond let the current sweep him toward the canoe. Quickly, he climbed back into the wooden sanctuary and continued his journey.

Water sprayed in his face. He saw alligators on the shore eyeing him quizzically as he navigated around several obstructions.

Finally, high above he saw what he'd been searching for—a mountainous rise shaped like a claw. He nearly howled in triumph as he fought to bring the canoe to shore.

Raymond began his journey skyward using the climbing tools he'd borrowed from camp. He had gone thirty feet up when his teeth started chattering. Raymond hated to stop, but he knew the consequences of forging ahead in such a state.

After dropping to a ledge, he stripped off his clothing and laid it out in the sun to dry. He had learned much by helping his father. When the body's temperature dropped too much, the cold could become deadly. Dr. Wilks had treated many poor souls who'd ignored their own bodies' warnings.

Finally, after thirty minutes or so, Raymond dressed in his newly dried clothes and resumed his ascent.

"Now we're getting somewhere," Raymond said, mindful to take his time and always check the strength of his handholds. His father had taught him this, as well, on one of their outings.

Raymond was halfway to his destination when impatience set in. Sweat poured into his eyes. Grabbing hold of the next ledge, he hauled himself up without first testing if the ledge could hold his weight.

There was a sharp crack, and suddenly, Raymond found himself pitched backward. His arms pinwheeled. He tried to find something to grab, but his hands clasped empty air and his feet slid from the rock.

A second later, he was falling. The ground reached up for Raymond, anxious to welcome him back. It all happened so fast, he had not even managed a scream.

Suddenly, a shape crowded into his tunneling vision. A field of amber, blue, and green surrounded him.

He struck, but it was not stone with which he connected. Instead, he felt something tough and leathery, yet comfortably pliant beneath him. The wind reached down and rustled his hair. The descent had ended. Unbelievably, he was on the rise once more.

With a gasp, he raised his head. He found himself looking down a long, graceful neck, toward the top of a beak longer than his entire body.

It was Windchaser. The Skybax had saved him!

He felt himself beginning to slide, but his body remembered Hikaro's lessons. He compensated with his weight, then reached out and grabbed hold of the Skybax's wings. The creature seemed shaky. The two rose and fell, gaining height as they arced around.

Raymond felt as if he might become dizzy.

The great stone claw of the mountain loomed up before them. The Skybax halted suddenly and pitched Raymond forward. He tumbled through empty air for the briefest of moments, then rolled onto a ledge until he came to a stop.

Laughter erupted from Raymond. Forgetting his nearly fatal fall, he was instead overjoyed by his ride.

He had done it! He had flown on Windchaser. Bareback, no less!

Turning, he saw Windchaser descend, blotting out the sun. The Skybax's wings seemed to glow with an impossible fire. Then they lowered, and the harsh glare of daylight was again in Raymond's eyes.

"Um, hello," Raymond said.

The Skybax let out a squall that hurt Raymond's ears. He winced at the painful sound, and the Skybax stopped suddenly.

"You saved my life," Raymond said, sensing Windchaser's barely contained anger.

Again, the hateful squall. The Skybax flapped its wings as if it might depart at any moment. The displaced air caused Raymond to stumble backward. Windchaser advanced on the boy he had saved, flapping his wings with a quiet menace.

Raymond swallowed nervously, not sure what to do. He turned his face from the Skybax and found himself looking into the cavern that Windchaser called home. The flapping of wings stopped suddenly. Raymond's eyes quickly adjusted to the near darkness.

He saw a crude painting on the wall of a young man's smiling face. It was a picture of Daniel, Windchaser's lost rider.

All about the cavern were reminders of Windchaser's loss. Raymond saw a backpack, an empty uniform, a cracked helmet, half-charred scrolls, a cup and saucer, a ball used for catching, and a sparkling clear stone hanging from a broken chain. Raymond guessed that all these items had belonged to Daniel. The rest of the cavern was bare.

"I've lost someone too," Raymond said without

turning. "And he meant everything to me. I know what it feels like."

Silence.

Finally, Raymond turned, worried that he would find the Skybax long gone. But Windchaser was not gone. He was still there, watching Raymond with an odd stare.

Raymond dropped to one knee and fished the pocketwatch from his boot. He set it down beneath the crystal droplet. "This was his. I'd like to keep it here, if that's all right."

Windchaser voiced no objection.

"You know the worst of it?" Raymond asked, surprised at the tears welling in his eyes. "There are days when I hate him for going away. It sounds strange, I'll admit. My father didn't ask to be killed. It wasn't his fault. He didn't want to be taken away. And I would give *anything* to have him back. But sometimes I'm more than just sad. Sometimes, I'm so...angry!"

The Skybax let out a mournful wail.

"Yes," Raymond said. In some impossible way, the sound made by the Skybax was the perfect expression of the pain and confusion in his own soul.

Suddenly, a noise came from the mouth of the cavern. Someone had dropped a rope down from above. A figure descended upon the rope and called out, "Raymond!"

With an angry cry, Windchaser whirled.

Though the figure was a silhouette, Raymond

knew that voice all too well.

"Hugh," he said hoarsely.

The Skybax headed toward Hugh with remarkable speed. Hugh started to climb up the rope and was nearly out of the way when the Skybax ripped past him and sailed out over the cliff's edge.

"Windchaser!" Raymond cried, but the Skybax did not return.

Hugh dropped back down to the mouth of the cavern. He approached Raymond, who met him halfway.

"What are you doing here?" Raymond asked angrily.

"Didn't you think anyone would miss you? Bix and me were worried you would get yourself killed. She figured out where you must have been going."

Raymond nodded, calming down. He looked to the rope.

"There's an easier way of finding this place," Hugh said. "Bix tried to make getting here sound impossible to keep you from trying it. She was trying to protect you."

Raymond walked to the ledge of the cavern and looked up. The Skybax circled overhead a few times, then flew off.

"Well, we'd better go," Hugh said. "My path may be shorter and less dangerous, but it will still take us time to get back."

Hugh watched as disappointment enshrouded his

friend. He was sorry about that, but he told himself that he was acting in Raymond's best interests. Still, a part of him knew the truth. A part of Hugh was secretly pleased that he'd come between Raymond and the Skybax.

Another part of him, however, was ashamed at what he had done.

Hugh looked around and noticed the odd shrine the Skybax had created with items kept from the rider he'd lost. It reminded Hugh of that doll he had almost taken from the girl in Waterfall City.

Anger suddenly flooded him. At times, it seemed all of Dinotopia was constructed for the sole purpose of making him feel like a complete *rotter*. He had been right to come and try to save Raymond from his own foolishness. And look at the thanks he was given!

Hugh whirled on Raymond, about to chastise his friend for acting so sullen and ungrateful. He stopped when he saw the same profound loss in his friend's eyes that he had first seen the night Raymond knew his father was dead.

"Come on," Hugh said softly. "Maybe if we stay out in the open for a time he'll come back."

"You think?" Raymond asked.

"Anything's possible," Hugh said, not really believing it. "Anything at all."

Raymond was in no mood for sleep when he returned to the dormitory. His mind was racing. His body, however, was exhausted, and he fell asleep quickly.

He dreamed of flying bareback on Windchaser, soaring over forgotten lands. Without warning, the dream transformed into a nightmare. Raymond found himself flying through a terrible storm. Looking beyond the magnificent stretch of the Skybax's wings, he saw the prison ship *Redemption* below. Father was on the bridge, fighting for his life.

The bearded man who had claimed the honor of killing the elder Wilks was struggling to push his father closer and closer to the ship's rail. Raymond screamed, his cry joined by that of the Skybax.

Bolting awake, Raymond heard Windchaser's distinctive cry. Was he still dreaming?

He looked around. None of the other students were stirring. Even Hugh was sound asleep. Odd, that no one else was disturbed by the sound. It must have come from his dream. Going outside would be pointless.

On the other hand, Raymond knew he would never go back to sleep until he was certain. After slipping from his warm bed, Raymond hurried out of the dormitory.

The night was a bit chilly, but Raymond was only aware of a strange hissing off to his right. He followed the sound until he came to a clearing. Suddenly, he heard massive wings beating in the darkness. Looking up, he saw Windchaser above, gliding in close for a landing.

The Skybax opened its beak and a strange whisper came from the creature. The sound was repeated several times until Raymond was certain the Skybax was calling his name.

Impossible!

Sollis had explained that no Skybax spoke conventional language. There was an instinctive understanding between a Skybax and rider. In all the years Saurians had existed in Dinotopia, no Skybax had ever displayed an ability to speak either Saurian or human language. Exactly how they communicated remained one of the island's greatest mysteries.

"Rrrrraaayyy-monnnnndd," Windchaser said as he cruised to the ground. *"Rayyyyyy-monnnnndd!"*

Now Raymond knew he was dreaming. And, yet, a part of him was certain he was wide awake. This was real. It was happening.

"I just want it to sound like my name," Raymond said, refusing to believe his senses.

"Stubbbborrnnnnn," Windchaser said, now on his feet.

Raymond's heart leaped into his throat. "Did you just say what I think you said?"

Windchaser cocked his huge head slightly to one side, as if to say *What do you think?*

"Oh, my," Raymond muttered. "You do understand me."

Windchaser brought his massive wings together several times, applauding his young, confused friend.

Raymond was not exactly certain if the applause was meant as a genuine congratulation or if the Skybax was teasing him. He suspected the latter.

"Am I the first you've spoken to?" Raymond asked.

Windchaser lowered his gaze and looked away.

"It was Daniel, wasn't it?" Raymond tried.

The Skybax whirled its head in Raymond's direction.

"He taught you," said Raymond.

Standing on his haunches, Windchaser fixed Raymond with a scornful gaze.

"No," Raymond said, understanding. "I suppose it was the other way around."

Windchaser nodded his head. *"Learnnnnn fasssssst."*

Raymond smiled. "I like to think so."

"Himmmmm," Windchaser said. *"Not youuuuuu."*

Clearing his throat, Raymond said, "I'll keep that in mind."

An odd racking sound came from the Skybax. At first, Raymond thought the creature was sick. He was about to call for help when it occurred to him that Windchaser was laughing!

"So is that why you came tonight?" Raymond asked, amazed at how quickly he was adjusting to the notion of a talking Skybax. "To make fun of me?"

Windchaser shrugged his wings, causing a slight breeze to kick up.

"I bet you're lonely," Raymond said. "I know I am."

Lowering his head slightly, Windchaser made an odd sound. The trilling that came from the Skybax seemed to be composed of several different sounds at once. How was such a thing possible?

He's speaking to me in his language, Raymond thought.

Windchaser's tones changed, becoming a complex series of musical movements. With such marvelous, complex sounds, Raymond could almost picture Windchaser and his fellow Skybaxes performing a formal recital in a great London hall.

"What is it you're trying to say to me?" Raymond asked.

The Skybax fell silent, then said, *"Lonelyyyy, I ammmmmm, toooooooo."*

"Have you spoken with anyone except me and Daniel?" Raymond asked.

Windchaser shook his head. Though he could speak the human language, the process was clearly difficult for him.

"Do all the Skybaxes understand us, or just you?"

The majestic, winged creature gave no indication that he would answer this question.

"You have this amazing gift," Raymond said. "Why don't you share it? Why don't you let everyone know? You're special! I bet there's never been a Skybax like you. Maybe there'll never be one again!"

Windchaser shook himself violently. He clearly rebelled at the very thought of sharing his gift with anyone except Raymond.

"Yyyyyou," Windchaser said. *"Otherssss, nnnnnot."* The Skybax beat his wings, preparing to run forward and lift himself into the air.

Raymond was seized by a sudden panic. He could not let Windchaser leave like this. "Wait, please! I won't tell anyone. I promise!"

The Skybax looked at him suspiciously. *"Nnnottt otherrrrr boyyy?"*

"Hugh? No, I won't tell him. I won't tell anyone. Please, you've got to believe me!"

The Skybax settled down.

Raymond did his best to calm himself. It was clear that Windchaser's bond with his previous rider had been so strong that the Skybax had overcome all barriers separating them. Raymond had to somehow prove himself to the Skybax—that he was worthy of the same.

"Teach me your language," Raymond said.

The Skybax stared in thought for a few long moments, then nodded in agreement.

Windchaser made a sound for Raymond.

The boy tried to duplicate it, but failed. He tried again. Then again. But no matter how hard he tried, he could not.

Windchaser shook his head. They made several

more attempts. This time the Skybax tried other sounds, simpler ones. Raymond concentrated and was finally able to mimic a few of them.

"So what does that mean?" Raymond asked, repeating the short string of tones. "Tell me, please!"

"*Sssoulll hasss whattt boddyyy lackkss,*" Windchaser said.

"I don't understand," Raymond said.

"*Waaattccchhhh.*"

The Skybax ran a short distance, unfurled its winged arms and leaped into the air. He glided swiftly by, then passed back again.

The breeze from his wings was sweet to Raymond, because with it came understanding. Those words were a simple riddle: What does a human soul have that an earthbound body lacks?

"Wings!" Raymond shouted.

With a cry of triumph, Windchaser descended to the ground and continued the lessons afresh. The Skybax seemed amused. Once again, he would have the opportunity to "train" a human.

CHAPTER 11

"Well," Bix said, "I heard about your little adventure. I'm relieved to see you in one piece."

Raymond shuffled uneasily. The morning had been spent participating in the weekly celebration for new inductees. In the afternoon, he had transferred his belongings to the second phase of Skybax Camp, the gold buildings.

After an introductory speech by Hikaro, who would follow the students through all three stages of the camp, Raymond was allowed several more hours of liberty. He found Bix with the cleanup crew in the central fairgrounds.

"I found him," Raymond told Bix. "I found Windchaser."

"So Hugh told me."

Raymond nodded. He was not surprised his friend had kept their adventure from everyone except the Protoceratops. "Bix, I need to make him understand."

"Understand what?" she asked patiently.

"That things can get better."

Bix stared intently at Raymond, then gave her blessing to his enterprise. "In the process of helping him, you may well heal yourself."

"I don't understand."

"You don't have to. Follow your heart, and all will be well." She looked up. "Why don't you invite him to help us?"

Raymond was startled. He glanced to the skies and saw Windchaser circling above. Waving his hands, Raymond signaled his friend to come down. Raymond honestly didn't think that Windchaser would accept his invitation.

But to Raymond's surprise, the Skybax was soon cruising to the ground. Several people and dinosaurs cleared the area uneasily. They looked to Bix for guidance. The sight of the small Protoceratops standing firm helped prevent panic.

Windchaser joined the humans and Saurians in their task of clearing the grounds. Raymond was with him constantly. Together they picked up debris and deposited it in a nearby cart.

After about an hour, a Skybax and rider came to the camp to deliver a message. Windchaser abandoned the cleanup duty and went over to the other Skybax.

Raymond watched the odd interplay between Windchaser and the messenger. At first, they seemed to be having a heated exchange. Then Windchaser turned and flew off.

Raymond ran from the fairgrounds, following the Skybax from below. At the edge of camp, Windchaser suddenly changed course. He circled directly above Raymond a few times, then landed close by him.

Rushing forward, Raymond wrapped his arms around Windchaser's head and soothingly caressed the clearly agitated creature. Both of them looked around to ensure that they were not observed.

"What is it?" Raymond asked, his heart thundering. "What did the Skybax say?"

"*Beginnn ttto tttrrrrainnn againnnnn. Jjjjoinnn withhh othherssss.*" Windchaser suddenly turned away. "*Affffraidddd.*"

"Don't be," Raymond said brightly. "I know just how we can start."

As evening came, many of the children were playing games in the fairgrounds. Raymond went to Hikaro, who was teaching them a Japanese rhyme.

"Honorable teacher," Raymond said. "I have a friend who would like to join in the games. May he?"

"Of course!"

Turning, Raymond hollered, "Windchaser!"

The children froze as the Skybax emerged from his hiding place behind one of the tents in the fairgrounds. Hikaro looked as if he might raise an objection at any moment, but he remained silent. He watched closely as the Skybax approached.

"Let us see," Hikaro said as he crossed his arms over his chest. "What game *could* your friend play with the others? He is a shade larger than they are."

Before Raymond could say anything, one of the children approached Windchaser. The young boy gently stroked the Skybax's head. A trilling sound expressed Windchaser's pleasure. He bent lower and was taken completely by surprise when the child leaped onto his neck!

Startled, the Skybax raised his head up, lifting the child high into the air.

Raymond was terrified that a sudden movement from Windchaser would send the boy flying. Instead, the child slid down Windchaser's back. He laughed, then cried out in delight as he hit the ground.

Windchaser looked toward the other children. They were all lining up for their turn!

On the edge of the fairgrounds, Bix and Hugh watched in amazement as the Skybax became a Saurian slide.

Windchaser was clearly pleased. He suddenly let out a call that sounded like a chorus of flutes. Everyone waited for several tense moments until the call was answered. A single reply. Two more.

In a few minutes, three other Skybaxes appeared. At first, Windchaser was shy in their presence. Then the games began again, and Windchaser was in the thick of things, playing and enjoying himself.

"And here I thought he was a bleedin' monster," Hugh said. Even Hugh's heart was lightened by the sight. Then, suddenly, Hugh's mood began to change as a frightening feeling of loss crept over him.

"Hugh," Bix said, sensing the sudden change in the boy. "Raymond will always be your friend. Perhaps Windchaser could be as well. After all, you and the Skybax seem to have quite a lot in common."

"In common? What do we have in common?" asked Hugh. But Bix said nothing more. She simply wandered off, leaving Hugh to ponder his own question.

The next day, Hugh was relieved to have some time away from his normal chores at the camp.

Besides Raymond and Bix, Hugh had made no real friends here. That had not been the fault of the Dinotopians.

The other Skybax handlers had been quite friendly to Hugh. There had been none of the coolness he had feared. He had been treated just like anyone else, despite being a newcomer.

So why didn't he *feel* like everyone else?

With a sigh, he tried not to think about this. Instead, he gazed at his surroundings.

This morning, he had been assigned what he considered guard duty. He was happy—it was very easy work. No work at all, actually. His task was simply to watch the high wire.

The wire had been strung between two tall platforms and located in a field off to the west of the final training area. Here students could get used to heights and hone their balance on the lines.

This morning the safety nets below had been removed for repair. For the next three days, the area would be a hazard. Hugh's job was to keep watch and make sure no one wandered into the dangerous area.

He scanned the bright, cheery, open field and was relieved to find no one in sight. He had no timepiece except the sun in the sky. After close to two hours of pacing and sitting, sitting and pacing, he began to dislike this simple assignment.

How much longer was he on duty, anyway? Would they leave him here for hours with nothing to keep him occupied except his own thoughts?

That might prove dangerous.

An urge he had resisted for days came upon him. Muttering a curse, Hugh reached into the pocket of his pants and withdrew a crumpled sheet of parchment. Memories flooded back as he unfolded the brittle page and stared at the writing.

The secret for turning base metal into gold.

In the outside world, such knowledge would make him a god among men. On Dinotopia, it made him no one special.

"Come on, O'Donovan. Throw it away," he told

himself. "You can do it. It's bloody well not going to do you any good here, and there's sure no way off this island. Not unless..."

He shuddered.

Not unless they were *lying* to him.

"Now you're really going around the bend, old friend. You're even *talking* to yourself, like some nit in the pages of a bloody Yank dime novel."

Hugh felt ashamed of his own thoughts. Nevertheless, all this friendliness and openness frightened him terribly. He was used to thinking of the world as divided between two kinds of people—those who made up the rules and those who followed them. And he knew exactly where people like him belonged in that grand division of things: slipping right between the cracks.

Suddenly, he was startled from his thoughts by a shrill scream. He spun, searching the grounds. Who had cried out? He saw no one.

Then he shifted his gaze upward. He saw a boy dangling from the high wire. If the boy fell, it would be fifty feet straight down. He wouldn't have a chance.

Hugh raised the horn he had been given to call for help. A loud, rich sound came from it as he ran toward the high wire. Abandoning the horn, Hugh leaped for the highest rung he could catch on the high wire's north ladder.

"Hang on!" he cried. His heart thundered and his every nerve was on fire. How could these Dinotopians have been so stupid? There were too many directions from which a stray boy or girl could wander into this area!

There should have been a fence, he thought angrily. Why did they put him, of all people, on this duty? They should have known better—

No, he suddenly demanded of himself. *Stop making excuses!*

"Help me! Please!" cried the boy hanging from the wire.

Hugh raced up to the platform, praying he would get there in time.

CHAPTER 12

Hugh was relieved to see the child holding on with both arms circling the wire. The boy's face was pale, his features twisted into a fearful mask.

"You're going to be all right!" Hugh said, suddenly feeling wobbly as he looked down. *The boy needs solid ground, not your stupid words*, he thought. *Help him!*

Drawing a steadying breath, Hugh took in the situation. The boy was six feet out onto the wire. Too far for Hugh to simply extend his hand and pull him back. How on earth was he going to save the boy?

Suddenly, a squall sounded from above. He glanced upward and saw a Skybax circling near the sun.

"Yes, come! Help us!" Hugh cried. He tried to catch sight of the Skybax again, but the sun's glare blinded him. He looked away, rubbing his eyes as fireworks seemed to dance before his vision. Then he scanned the sky again.

He saw nothing. *Where did that Skybax go?*

"I'm scared!" the boy shouted.

So am I, thought Hugh.

He had to think of something fast. The child looked as if he might lose his grip any moment now. Seconds ticked by, and Hugh felt frozen in his tracks, completely useless!

Finally an idea came to him. Maybe he could allow himself to dangle from the line. Then he could move toward the boy by climbing hand over hand. The boy could cling to Hugh's neck as he took them back.

Hugh froze again. What if the added tension on the line caused a vibration? It could make the boy lose his hold.

Blood and thunder, the boy might fall no matter what he did! But he had to try something!

"I'm slipping!" the child screamed.

"Just hold on!" Hugh snarled impatiently, immediately regretting his harsh tone. "I'll save you! I will!"

Hugh crouched down and tried to reach out for the wire. His hands were trembling and he could not make himself take the line.

Do it, he thought. *You have to!*

The tips of his fingers touched the wire in time to feel it vibrate in his hands. He heard a scream!

The boy had fallen!

He watched the impossibly fast descent, and was amazed that the child wasn't screaming. Had he passed out?

Don't look, don't look! a voice inside Hugh warned, but he could not tear his gaze away.

A sudden gust of wind struck him and nearly blew him off the platform.

A Skybax dove toward the ground at an impossible speed. The boy was perhaps fifteen feet from disaster when the Skybax swept under him. It scooped him up, breaking his fall.

Hugh cheered as the Skybax sailed a few hundred feet, then glided to a landing. It gently deposited the fallen child onto the ground. A group of people raced toward the child and his rescuer.

Hugh's burst of happiness was over in a heartbeat as he remembered his own failure. With a heavy heart, he began the long climb down to the ground.

He did not see Windchaser circling the area above and watching everything with keen interest.

Much later, Raymond found Hugh in a secluded area almost a mile from camp. The older boy sat at the edge of a small pond.

"How did you know where to look?" Hugh asked.

"A Skybax Rider saw you heading this way. I had a feeling you wouldn't go too far."

"Why did you bother? Haven't you heard what I did? I was too much of a coward to save that boy."

Raymond sat beside his friend. "But the boy was saved."

"The people here knew I was a troublemaker. Now they must think I'm a worthless coward. I don't belong here, and this just proves it."

"That's not true at all—" Raymond began.

"But it is!" Hugh interrupted as he withdrew a crumpled sheet of parchment from his pocket and handed it to his friend. "I never want to see this again."

Raymond saw the formula on the page. "This again."

"Yes," Hugh said. "If I hadn't been daydreaming about how rich and powerful those symbols would make me in the real world, none of this would have happened. Just goes to show, some people don't deserve the trust they're given."

"Why are you so unhappy here?" Raymond asked.

"Because I don't belong in Dinotopia! For a time, I held a speck of hope that somehow I could fit in here. But I was wrong. Hope is the enemy back where I come from. There was a saying there: Those who sit around on the street dreaming that things will get better are more likely to be hit by a wagon!"

Raymond shook his head. "You're wrong, Hugh. Hope matters. Trying matters."

Hugh would not look his friend in the eye. "You don't understand. I thought Dinotopia was different—and it is—but *I'm* not. What happened today proved that. I'm sorry, Raymond, but I'm not good enough for this place. The dolphins made a mistake. They should have left me to drown."

A rustling sound came from a nearby cluster of trees. Bix suddenly stepped forward. She'd been listening all along. "I beg to differ," she broke in. "You saved Raymond's life!"

"That was different," Hugh said, not surprised at all by Bix's sudden appearance. By now Hugh had gotten used to Dinotopians appearing almost magically out of thin air.

"How was saving Raymond different?" Bix asked.

"I didn't have any time to think about that. A storm was raging! Daggers and cutlasses were flying. I just did it. This time I had to make a decision—put myself at risk or let someone else die. I couldn't do it. If that Skybax and his rider hadn't rescued the boy, he would have been killed."

Bix shook her head. "You should not be so hard on yourself. There are always second chances. Especially on Dinotopia."

"Second chances? Not for people like me," Hugh said, turning from his friends and walking away.

Raymond started to go after him.

"Don't," Bix said. "Hugh needs some time alone. He'll be fine."

Raymond watched Hugh's departing form and wished he could believe that.

The next day, a celebration was held to honor the bravery of the Skybax and rider who had saved the young boy. Hugh was there, but he watched only from the edge of the fairgrounds. He was half-hidden behind a large tree, well beyond the crowd.

In his mind, the coolness he had expected from the Dinotopians had finally arrived. He had been taken off guard duty for good. Hugh knew it was nothing less than he deserved. Why should they trust him to fail again?

He dreaded the looks he sometimes got from the people he had come to admire. Raymond claimed it was all in Hugh's own mind. But Hugh believed he knew people better than Raymond did!

All his life Hugh had been nothing more than a gutter rat. Being loathed was part and parcel of his former existence. If only the Dinotopians *hated* Hugh, then he would know what to do—hate right back! But this was far worse.

They didn't hate him. They pitied him. He just knew it!

The sidelong glances they gave him seemed to say, "He can't help himself. He's just a worthless Dolphinback."

Yes, he thought. *And a coward.*

One thing was clear to Hugh—he didn't deserve friends like Raymond and Bix. Come nightfall, he was going to leave Skybax Camp.

Backing away, Hugh heard a sharp cry. He spun and saw that he had stepped on the foot of a girl. She was about his own age and quite pretty, with short black hair and Asian features.

She smiled broadly. For a moment, Hugh found himself staring dumbly at the dark color of her eyes.

Chiding himself, he downturned his gaze, muttered an apology, and started to walk away.

"Oh, so that's how it is," she said. "Step on my toes, then act as if I mean nothing to you. I swear, boys on this island are all the same."

Hugh stopped abruptly and took another look at the young woman. There was something very different about her. "Are you Hikaro's daughter?"

"Hah!" she said. "He's Japanese. I'm *Chinese*. Big difference."

"Sorry."

"No need. I just didn't want to miss my chance to meet the *terrible* Hugh O'Donovan."

"Terrible," he said. "Yes, I suppose I am at that—"

She frowned. "I was teasing you! You know, joking..." She looked him up and down. "It is as I was told, you are all too serious. You must learn to have more fun in life!"

"Oh?" Hugh wondered who this girl was. "You have me at a disadvantage."

"You mean I know your name and you don't know mine. Lian."

"A pleasure," he said, bending slightly. He resisted the urge to kiss her hand as he might have done back in London. She looked as if she knew what he was about to do. She seemed disappointed when he did not follow his instincts.

"I am so happy to finally meet a Dolphinback!"

she said. "I love the Dinotopians, but it's not the same as a newcomer like you."

"Really?" he asked. "You do know that I'm considered a troublemaker."

"Of course! That's also why I wanted to meet you. Mind you, I've created my fair share of mischief, too. I'm leaving camp today, but I hope to see you again."

"You do?" he asked with happy disbelief.

"Sure," she said. "Why not?"

Hugh paused a moment, then looked away. "See that boy?" he asked, indicating the child standing on the stage at the center of the fairgrounds. The Skybax and rider who saved him stood at his side. "If that Skybax and rider hadn't arrived when they did, that child wouldn't be alive right now."

"I know all about it," Lian said, eyeing Hugh carefully.

Hugh was about to say something when Lian spoke again. "Will you do something for me?"

"Maybe."

"It won't be difficult, I promise. I would tell you to look to the future, but first you must accept the present," said Lian.

"I don't understand."

"Close your eyes."

"I—"

"Don't argue," she said.

Sighing, Hugh did as he was told.

"Now don't say anything," Lian whispered into his ear. "Just listen. Be calm. Take it all in. The heat upon your face, the soft breeze, the sounds of the crowd. Listen."

Hugh wondered what magic this young woman possessed. He obeyed her every command.

"Breathe deep," she said softly. "Seek peace."

For the first time since the near accident, Hugh felt calm. He heard the distinctive cry of a Skybax in the distance.

His mind reached back to the high wire. He had heard a Skybax then, too. It had been circling above, then it had vanished.

It had vanished for a long time, now that he thought about it. Several minutes had ticked by before the Skybax dived down to save the falling child.

The cry of the Skybax on the stage came again.

Suddenly, Hugh understood the mistake he had made. His eyes flashed open. "Lian!"

She was no longer beside him. Jasmine, the fragrance she had worn, lingered in the air. Of the young woman herself, there was no trace.

Hugh had no time to worry about Lian's magical disappearance. He had something more important to deal with.

As the ceremony proceeded, Hugh cut through the crowd and found Raymond.

"There were *two* Skybaxes," Hugh said.

Raymond looked at him strangely. "Pardon?"

"When I was on the platform I heard a Skybax. I looked up and saw one circling. Then it was gone."

"I don't see—"

"Windchaser! The Skybax I heard the first time sounded nothing like the one who saved the boy. Listen to it!"

Raymond nodded and listened to the caw made by the Skybax on the stage. "He doesn't sound a bit like Windchaser."

"That's right. But I wasn't thinking about that before. Windchaser must have been worried that he couldn't fly well enough to save the child on his own. He went and got help."

Raymond shook his head in wonder.

"I understand why *I'm* not being honored," Hugh said. "But Windchaser should be. That Skybax and rider didn't just show up. Windchaser brought them!"

Stunned, Raymond swore he would help Hugh reveal the truth. Together they made their way through the crowd and found Hikaro, who was standing close to the stage. He listened as Hugh spoke.

"Yes, we know about this," Hikaro said as he took the boys aside. "These honors were offered to Windchaser. He refused them."

"Why?" Raymond asked.

"I do not know," Hikaro said. "When I saw him playing with the children, I was encouraged. I thought he might be finding acceptance of his new life. Now, I am not so certain."

Hikaro was called back to the ceremony. Raymond and Hugh watched the conclusion of the honors.

"This isn't right," Hugh said.

Raymond nodded. "No, it isn't."

"What do you think we should do about it?"

"The only thing we *can* do," Raymond said. "Talk to Windchaser."

CHAPTER 13

Late that night, the boys made the journey to Windchaser's lair. As they had feared, Windchaser's home was deserted.

"Nothing's left," Hugh said, holding his lantern high. "He took everything that belonged to that other boy you told me about."

"Daniel."

"Even the picture on the wall has been obscured. It's as if he couldn't stand looking at it any more."

Raymond shook his head, desperate to force away the tears threatening to fall. "I still don't believe it. He wouldn't have just left like this. Not without..."

"Not without saying good-bye?" Hugh asked.

"Yes."

"Don't be so sure. I wasn't going to."

Raymond looked stunned. "What do you mean?"

"I didn't want to stay here after what happened. I thought I would do what I always do—run away."

Raymond was silent. He did not look at his friend.

Hugh put his hand on Raymond's shoulder.

"I'm sorry," Hugh said.

The younger boy shrugged off Hugh's hand and said, "Come on. We're wasting time here."

Suddenly, Hugh saw a glint of light in the corner. Crouching down, he saw the crystal that had belonged to Daniel. The pocketwatch Raymond's father had given him lay beside it.

"Look at this," Hugh said, picking up the crystal.

Raymond bent low and picked up the pocketwatch. He felt thoroughly rejected.

"This is an odd shape," Hugh said as he handled the crystal shard. "Like a teardrop."

"What difference does it make?" Raymond said, swatting the crystal from Hugh's hand. It fell against a rock and shattered.

Raymond ran to the lip of the cavern's entrance and whipped his hand back, ready to throw the pocketwatch into the ravine. But there was nothing in his hand. Turning, he saw Hugh holding the watch.

"I told you I was the best pickpocket in all of London," Hugh said. "If you want, I'll hold on to it for a while."

"I don't care what you do with it. You were right. Everyone goes away. *Everyone.*"

"I'm still here," Hugh said. "Does that count?"

Raymond frowned and hung his head low. With a wordless apology, he reached out and took back the pocketwatch. The moment it was in his hand, he felt as he always had when holding it—as if a part of his father was still with him.

They returned to camp in silence.

The next day, Bix approached Raymond as the boy walked back to the dormitories after class.

"He's been seen," Bix said.

"Windchaser?"

"Yes. But it was far from here, and he's not likely to return."

"Tell me where," Raymond said. "Please."

The Protoceratops lowered her head. "I cannot. I have not forgotten what happened the last time. Where he has gone, you may not follow. It is a special retreat. The way is far too dangerous. I am so sorry."

Raymond pleaded with Bix to tell him, but the dinosaur's resolve was firm. Soon they parted. Raymond felt crushed.

As he walked to the dormitories alone, he thought about the previous night. He had to figure out where Windchaser had gone. Maybe there was some clue sitting in Windchaser's lair.

He pictured everything he and Hugh had seen. That's when he thought of the crystal. He had seen a crystal like that once before. But where?

The answer came to him at once. He turned and ran back to the training area.

He found Hikaro wading through a mountain of scrolls. His instructor seemed grateful for the interruption.

Raymond talked with Hikaro about everything except what was on his mind. He didn't want anyone to guess he was going after Windchaser, no matter what. After nearly twenty minutes had passed, he casually mentioned the tear-shaped crystal that Hikaro kept on his desk.

"This?" the instructor asked as he picked up the crystal. "They are sometimes given as tokens of achievement when one becomes a Skybax Rider."

"It doesn't look so special," Raymond said.

"Perhaps to you, but on Dinotopia there is only one place that has such crystals. Once a crystal is given, the Skybax and his rider must make a pilgrimage to that place. It is a special retreat called the Sky Galley Caves."

A retreat—exactly what Bix had described! Surely he could find Windchaser there. Rather than shouting in triumph, Raymond simply shrugged and carefully changed the subject. Raymond knew that Hugh himself would be impressed with this artful performance!

Soon, Hikaro begged Raymond's forgiveness and said he had to return to his work.

"*Arigatoo gozaimashita,*" Raymond said, conveying a proper thank-you in Japanese. He had learned it secretly to please his teacher. It worked.

"*Doomo arigatoo gozaimashita,*" Hikaro replied, with a look of happy surprise.

Raymond left the training buildings and raced to the dormitory, where Hugh was waiting.

"The Sky Galley Caves!" Raymond said. "That's where he's gone."

"In the Forbidden Mountains?"

"Yes!" Raymond delighted in explaining how he had acquired the knowledge.

"If one didn't know better, one might think you've been cavortin' with a bad sort," Hugh said with a laugh. "You're becoming a regular dodger!"

"He's there," Raymond said. "I know it!"

A ragged breath escaped Hugh. "Then I suppose we have seen the last of him."

Raymond's eyes widened. "You're joking, right?"

"No," Hugh said.

"But we can't give up."

Hugh swallowed hard. "Raymond, I know this means the world to you, but let me just say two bleedin' words: Tyrannosaurus rex."

Raymond spun on his friend. "Really? Well, let me say two *bleedin'* words: Who cares? Windchaser's my friend, and I'm not giving up."

Hugh stared at Raymond, startled by the force behind his words. Hugh allowed a wicked smile to spider across his face. "Tell me somethin'. If it had been *me* that had run off, would you risk being eaten by a bleedin' Tyrannosaurus just to know I was safe?"

Raymond answered without hesitation. "Yes."

"Well," Hugh said with a sigh. His smile had not faded. "That does make things interesting, now, doesn't it?"

"I suppose."

"So you want to break the rules," Hugh said, his eyebrow arched. "Just run off without telling anyone? Forget the consequences?"

"Yes," Raymond said.

Hugh laughed. "There may be hope for you yet, dodger. When do we leave?"

CHAPTER 14

"Tell me again," Hugh said as they climbed a series of rocks.

"Tyrannosaurus rex isn't evil," explained Raymond. "They're just hungry."

"Right," said Hugh.

"They're also not stupid. Far from it."

"That part I could live without hearing over and over," said Hugh.

"You can negotiate with them if need be."

"Really?" Hugh sighed. "I suppose it might help if we had something to negotiate *with*."

"I'm not worried," said Raymond.

"I am!"

The boys were two days into their journey. They had stowed aboard a supply wagon headed north and were now well on their way to the Forbidden Mountains.

"It's getting colder," Hugh said, almost out of breath. "And it shouldn't be so dark."

"Storm clouds," Raymond said a bit nervously.

"They've been following us."

"Oh, good," Hugh said. "That's bloody wonderful."

"I'm not worried."

"You said that."

Raymond shrugged. He had read about a way to make a safe crossing through the Forbidden Mountains. There was a land bridge the carnivores avoided. The author of the scroll Raymond had found guessed that Tyrannosaurus rex avoided the bridge because of their own superstitions.

Ahead lay a rocky vista—gray stone slabs, sharp rises, and twisting paths that sometimes led in great circles. Raymond and Hugh had packed provisions to last them a week. As night fell, they began to wonder if they should have brought more.

Hugh built a small fire, and they huddled before it. The rain was still a ways off, but the cold was now upon them. They had taken no sweaters or coats.

Hugh was shivering as he said, "You realize what we're doing is beyond stupidity. I mean, we don't know for certain that Windchaser is at the Sky Galley Caves. Or what to expect when we get there."

Raymond raised one eyebrow. "What's your point?"

Before Hugh could respond, a crackling came from the darkness behind them.

"What was that?" Hugh demanded.

"Probably not a carnivore. We won't have to worry about them until we cross the bridge tomorrow."

"Comforting," Hugh muttered.

Another sound came—a twig being broken much farther away.

"Whatever it is, it's moving off," Raymond said.

"Or going back to get the rest of the dinner party."

Yawning, Raymond said, "Well, if that's your attitude, maybe you should take the first watch. I'm going to sleep."

"You can't sleep now! We might be in danger."

"If we are, we'll deal with it," Raymond said as he brushed away a handful of stones from the ground and lay down.

"How?"

"By running for our lives, probably," Raymond said as he turned over and immediately drifted off to sleep.

Hugh was dragging himself the next morning. The sky was steel gray, and winds hissed through the narrow passages between the great stone walls surrounding the boys. They were moving slower now. The path had become more dangerous.

The two made their way along a ledge overlooking a ravine. Both knew very well that laziness could get them killed. They tested the path ahead with extreme care, securing each handhold with serious concentration.

Hugh's nerves were becoming frayed. "You know,"

he said, "Laegreffon had a saying. *'There is always more than one road to any given destination.'* What I mean, Raymond, is that there might be an easier way than this."

"Fine. *You* take us there!"

"I'm just saying…"

"I know, Hugh, I know."

"You don't think it was a sabertooth, do you?" asked Hugh. "If they still exist."

Raymond shook his head. "I doubt it. On both counts."

"So what did we hear last night?"

"I don't know. It could have been anything. All that matters is that it didn't want to have anything to do with us. Now keep quiet. I can't concentrate."

That afternoon, the rain began. At first it was a mild drizzle, then it turned into a torrent. They had navigated past the most dangerous paths on the cliff-side. Turning a sharp corner, they saw safety looming fifteen feet away. The ledge ended just ahead and a clearing was in plain view.

An unspoken agreement passed between them. They could dig in where they were and hope the winds would stop soon. But both of them knew that the storm was growing stronger. Their situation would get worse before it got better. They had to keep moving.

The rain seemed to slice through them. Thunder rumbled and lightning flashed. Suddenly, a sound ripped across the mountain pass, echoing from one wall to the other.

Hugh saw it before Raymond did. A boulder was falling ahead of them. First it struck the ledge, then it slid into the wide space separating their path from the one on the cliffside opposite. The gap was no more than twenty feet across.

Neither boy could hear the boulder strike the turbulent channel below. The wail of the storm muted the sound of the rock's landing.

Hugh reached out and put his hand on Raymond's shoulder. Then he leaned in close so he could scream in Raymond's ear. "This is crazy! We're going to get ourselves killed!"

Raymond turned and shouted into Hugh's ear, "I can see the clearing again! The storm's lightening up!"

Hugh noticed that the rain was lessening slightly. "So let's wait!"

"No!"

Raymond yanked himself away from his friend, his arms suddenly pinwheeling in the air. He steadied himself and took another step.

Hugh saw a clump of roots jutting from between two great stones. He grabbed them for support and moved to follow his friend.

A blinding light filled his vision. Heat struck him. A sizzling engulfed him.

Lightning!

The brilliance faded, and Hugh saw Raymond

staring at him. Raymond's eyes bulged. His face was ashen.

"That hit too close!" Raymond said. "If we were in the clearing, it might have gone for the tallest object. Us!"

"So we stay?"

"You bet we stay. I haven't seen a gale like this one since the night my father—"

A loud cracking noise suddenly sounded from above. Instinctively, Hugh reached out for Raymond, but the boy twisted and looked up.

A mass of debris had come loose from the high rocks. Both boys watched as a monstrous shape moved swiftly past them. Hugh had his hand on Raymond's shirt as the gnarled branch of a falling tree reached out and hooked itself around Raymond's left arm.

Fear tore through Hugh as he watched Raymond lose his footing and start to fall. The former thief held on to his friend's shirt, but the fabric ripped and Raymond was carried from him, down into the crevasse.

Hugh screamed, but the sound was swallowed up by the storm.

CHAPTER 15

I haven't seen a gale like this one since the night my father—

Raymond's words echoed in Hugh's mind. He knew how Raymond would have completed the statement.

—the night my father was killed.

Hugh stood on the ledge of the mountain, staring into the gray sky. He could not believe that he had lost his friend.

Why had he agreed to any of this? he asked himself. Why had he not left Skybax Camp the other night, as he had planned?

You know the answer, he thought.

Hugh came because of what he had seen in Raymond's eyes. He knew that look. He had seen it in the mirror enough times. Raymond was fiercely determined to see the Sky Galley Caves. Raymond would have gone anyway—with or without his friend.

Hugh had come to keep Raymond safe. Besides,

Hugh had his own unfinished business with Wind-chaser. Now it would remain unfinished forever.

The downpour was letting up. Hugh could not move. He knew he had to begin the long journey back to camp, where he would try to explain what had happened. He had failed to keep his friend safe. Raymond was dead. They had come here—to the Forbidden Mountains...to Dinotopia—for nothing!

Then he heard a sound. It came from just below the ledge.

Crouching, Hugh looked out onto the ravine below. An impossible sight greeted him. The tree that had dragged Raymond over the edge had not fallen into the waters below. It was large enough so that it had become wedged between the cliffsides about fifty feet below the ledge.

The remainder of the fallen debris had created a sort of bridge across the divide. Raymond lay cradled in the tree's branches, horribly still. Hugh thought he could see blood upon the lad's temple. His limbs were resting at odd angles.

Was he dead? Or was he still alive?

"Raymond!" Hugh called. "Raymond, can you hear me?"

Hugh held his breath as he felt a strong updraft of wind against his cheek. There! He saw Raymond shift slightly.

His friend was alive!

Hugh's elation was snatched away from him as he

saw the entire structure holding Raymond sag sharply. The bridge fell half a foot, then stopped.

The drop to the stream below was at least a thousand feet!

"Steady," Hugh said softly, worried to speak any louder. If Raymond continued to move about, he might bring the entire structure crashing down.

Think, think, think, Hugh demanded of himself. There must be a way to get down to Raymond, to get him out.

The slight break that had come in the storm abruptly ended. Rain began to fall again. It was much lighter this time, but still steady.

In horror, Hugh saw the tree begin to slip again.

A sound came from Hugh's left. He turned sharply but could see nothing.

It was a strange thumping and scratching sound. What could it be?

Hugh was certain of only one thing—he had heard this sound last night, just before taking the watch. Some creature was following them. And it was closing in fast.

He looked around for a weapon. A heavy branch was lying nearby. Hugh picked it up and brandished it, hoping he would look like enough of a threat to put off whatever was coming. *Hoping,* but not really believing.

Suddenly, a voice within Hugh began shouting. He recognized it as a voice from his past. It was the voice of selfish survival—the one he'd always listened to back on the London streets. *Save yourself! The clearing is fifteen feet away. You won't be able to help Raymond if you bloody well get yourself eaten!*

But this was betrayal. It was no different from what that bloke did to Hugh back in London. He'd called himself Hugh's friend, yet he had turned Hugh in for a reward.

That was the way of things back there, thought Hugh. But not here. And not inside him. Not anymore.

In a heartbeat, Hugh made his decision. If their positions were reversed, Raymond would never abandon him. No matter the danger, no matter the consequences, Hugh would not leave his friend.

The sounds came again. Louder this time. Closer. A darkness fell directly before him, its shape obscured by the gray curtain of rain.

Suddenly he heard an ear-piercing squall. He was so startled that he dropped the branch and nearly lost his balance. An alien shape moved in, pushing through the veil of rain as if it were parting curtains. Two reddish eyes immediately came into view, along with a beak the length of a man.

Windchaser!

The rain slowed again, allowing Hugh a better look at the Skybax. Now he knew what he'd been hearing—the sound of ten-foot-long Skybax legs trying to tiptoe closer!

"Down there!" Hugh cried as he pointed toward Raymond.

The Skybax looked over the ledge, then drew back in horror when he saw Raymond's terrible situation.

Windchaser's head shook violently, then he hesitated, as if weighing his options. He looked down again, then back to Hugh, cocking his head to one side imploringly.

"What are you waiting for?" Hugh asked. "Fly down there and save him!"

The Skybax's only movement was the agitated twisting of his long neck.

"There isn't much time! What's holding him in place may slip!"

With a violent shudder, Windchaser snapped, *"Yessssss! I sssssseeeee thhhatttt!"*

Hugh was startled by the Skybax's ability to speak. He had been told time and again that no Skybax possessed this skill.

"Wwwwasssss folllowwwinngggg. Wwanntted to fffffrightennnn yoouuuu bbbotthhhh. Mmmmake yooooouuu ttttturrrn bbbbbackkkkk."

Hugh's expression hardened. "You didn't do a very good job of it, did you?"

Suddenly, the shaky bridge beneath Raymond shifted again. More debris began to fall.

Hugh felt his blood turn to ice.

It wouldn't be long now. The bridge would soon be crumbling!

"I can't get to Raymond," Hugh cried. "All you've got to do is fly down and grab him!"

"*Nnnnnooooo!*" Windchaser cried. "*Cannnnnnot hollllld himmm. Youuuu mmmmusssst hellllp!*"

Hugh looked long and hard at the damaged membrane of the Skybax's wings. Some places were so thin they appeared translucent. Others were ragged and frayed—scar tissue from the burns Windchaser had suffered. Part of the creature's long right arm looked as if it had been broken and not reset before it knitted and the bones fused.

Finally, Hugh understood. It was a miracle that Windchaser could fly at all. If the Skybax got too close to Raymond, he could easily pitch the boy into the abyss by accident.

"We've got to do something!" Hugh said. He closed his eyes and tried to think. "If we had some rope, we could tie one end to you and the other to me. You could lower me down. I could grab Raymond. But what would we use?"

Luckily, the rain had stopped completely. The Skybax was able to rise into the air and fly off.

Hugh waited, staring down at Raymond.

When a squall sounded from the clearing, Hugh made his way off the ledge. He saw Windchaser nodding toward a pile of vines before he flew off again.

"Well, O'Donovan," Hugh said as he examined the strength of the vines. "Just like the old days.

Climbing down from rooftops, sneaking through windows."

Hugh drew the small blade he had packed and got to work cutting and interweaving the vines. Windchaser came back three times, dropping off more vines with each visit. But both of them soon realized that the vines were much too short. There was no way to quickly make a fifty-foot rope that would hold the weight of two boys.

"Well," said Hugh. "If we can't use the vines to lower me to Raymond, then we'll have to use them another way. I'll lash myself to your back, like a rider. I've seen it done at camp. 'Course they have bleedin' equipment for these matters. We'll just have to make do."

Windchaser agreed to Hugh's idea of lashing himself to the Skybax. Together they'd fly down and try to save Raymond.

"These should hold," he said, testing the strength of the vines he had already tied together. He guessed they were strong enough to support his weight, but he had no way of knowing if they would be able to take the stress for long. Also, what if Raymond's added weight was too much for them?

You'll "what if" yourself to death, O'Donovan, he thought. *There's no time!*

"All right," Hugh said. "Now, you fly underneath and—"

"Wwwwonnnn'tttt rrrreachhhh hhhhhimmm!"

Hugh thought about it and saw Windchaser's point. Flying underneath the tree bridge would do little good. They would not be able to get at Raymond since he lay on top.

"Yyyyourrr bbbackkkk to mmmmyyyy bbbellllyyyy," Windchaser said.

A chill raced through Hugh. He understood the Skybax's plan. Hugh would be lashed to Windchaser's underside, facing down into the abyss. His arms and legs would dangle, allowing him to snatch up Raymond as Windchaser glided through the gap.

Of course, if the vines broke or simply came undone, Hugh would drop like a stone.

"Let's get started," Hugh said, not wanting to think about what could happen.

Windchaser said, *"Nnnnottt llikkkee yyooouuu mmmuccchhhh."*

"Gee thanks," Hugh said dryly as he tied one end of the tangled vines around Windchaser's thick neck. "I'll try not to yank too hard and strangle you."

"Wwwwasssss aaaffrrraiiddd yoooouuuu."

"You were afraid of me?" Hugh said. "Why would you be afraid of me?"

"Aaaffrraidd tttaakkkke Rrrraaayyymmonnnd awwwwayyyyyy!!!" Windchaser said, his voice reflecting a genuine grief. *"Llllikkke Ddddannniellll."*

"Take him away? Like Daniel?" Hugh asked.

"Daniel's dead. I saved Raymond's life once! I would never hurt him."

"Nnnnnotttt unnnderrrstanndd!"

"We have no time for this," Hugh said as he finished his preparations. The harness he created fit loosely around the Skybax. Hugh slipped into the harness. He drew the vine ropes tight around his body.

"All right," Hugh said, "now give me some warning before—"

Hugh's words melted into a scream as Windchaser took a running jump and lifted him high into the air.

CHAPTER 16

Hugh watched in horror as the earth was snatched out from under him. He wanted to close his eyes, but he knew he had to quickly get used to this. For a moment he tried to imagine that he had sprouted wings and had been given the gift of flight.

The soft ground twenty feet below suddenly gave way as they flew past the edge of the clearing. Any comfort that might have been within Hugh's grasp raced away as he looked into the gap. The mountain walls on either side descended in a rush toward the churning waters waiting at the base of the great drop.

Windchaser took them above the tree bridge holding Raymond in place. The Skybax struggled to maintain his position. He lurched from side to side, rising and falling dramatically.

Hugh felt dizzy. "You're not going to pass out, you're not going to pass out," he chanted.

"Issssss yyyooouuuu I'mmmm worrrrrieddd abbboutttt," Windchaser said.

Hugh did not have the strength to tell the Skybax

that he was talking to himself. Suddenly, it occurred to him that the Skybax had a sense of humor as dark as his own.

"Just fly straight," Hugh muttered.

If Windchaser heard, he gave no indication. Instead, he began his sporadic descent, falling a few feet at a time, rocking sharply. The vines bit into Hugh's flesh, and he did his best to ignore the pain.

"*A ssssstrrronggg Sssssskyyyyybaxxxxx cannnn carrrrryyyyyy wwwwweighttttt of a mannnnnnn,*" Windchaser said. "*Immmm notttt ssssoooo sssstrrrronggg. Hhhhhope yyyyyyouuu hhhhhavvvennn'tttt bbbeeennnnn eattttinggg ttoooo mucccchhhhh!*"

"Bleedin' hilarious," Hugh groused, his stomach heaving at the Skybax's jerky movements. "Just get down close enough so's I can grab Raymond."

Hugh glanced down at Raymond. The boy was unconscious.

"We can't lose him. You know that, don't you? Neither of us can bear to lose him."

The Skybax did not reply.

The tree wedged between the cliffsides slipped again. This time it dropped on its right flank, where Raymond was nestled in a cradle of branches. The boy rolled over once, twice, then came to a stop.

Hugh was breathing hard. This had to work! But what if it didn't?

Don't think about that! he screamed to himself as thunder resounded through the mountains, and the clouds threatened to unleash yet another downpour.

"A little faster, why don't ya?" Hugh cried in frustration with Windchaser's slow descent.

Suddenly, they dove to within a few feet of Raymond. Hugh cried out in fear and felt one of the vines loosen slightly.

"Slower, slower!" Hugh yelped. He reached out and could almost touch Raymond. He could see the gash on the boy's forehead.

Raymond will be all right, Hugh kept telling himself.

"I can almost reach him," Hugh said. "Just come down a little bit."

The strong updraft of mountain winds filled Windchaser's wings. The Skybax adjusted his position and dropped dramatically. Hugh felt a bonelike finger of wood poke at his chest and suddenly he was on top of Raymond.

The Skybax wailed. Its efforts to regain its balance made the situation worse. The heavy tree forming the bony skeleton of the makeshift bridge tilted from side to side and started to sag.

Hugh reached out and flung his arms around Raymond, praying he had a firm enough grasp on his friend. They boy moaned slightly, his head dropping back.

"I've got him! I've got him! Go, go, go!" Hugh shouted.

Windchaser tried to pull up and failed. Instead,

they crashed down into the tangle of branches. Hugh heard a sharp scraping. He looked to his left in time to see the shattered tree trunk lose its hold on the side of the mountain.

Again, Hugh felt the world yanked out from under him. They were falling! Raymond's shirt was caught on the branches. Hugh felt his friend being dragged from his arms!

Within Hugh's mind, an all-too-familiar voice screamed at him to let go of Raymond. He and the Skybax would surely die if he didn't!

Hugh held on tight.

The Skybax wailed as all three plunged toward the icy waters below, dragged along by the remains of the fallen tree. The rest of the debris trapped in the network of branches was shaken loose. Bits of earth and stone flew toward the rapidly nearing waters.

Windchaser flapped his wings in desperation, but his efforts were wasted.

Hugh managed to control his panic long enough to move his hand to Raymond's shirt and pull. A hole opened in the material. Widened. Began to tear.

He yanked again, and tore through the seam. Raymond grunted as Hugh pulled him closer, hugging him tighter. The tear split through the remnants of Raymond's shirt, and it fell from his body.

The branch still held the shirt, but Raymond was free!

The tree spun away and slammed against the

left flank of the gap. It continued to fall as the Skybax's frantic efforts slowed their descent.

"Windchaser!" Hugh cried. "Get us out!"

The Skybax attempted to regain its balance. Instead, its efforts dragged them into the opposite side of the crevasse. Hugh saw the wall approaching and feared that both he and Raymond would be crushed on impact.

Somehow, Windchaser pirouetted, allowing his own back to slam against the stone wall.

They hit twice more before the Skybax managed to arrest their flight for the barest of instants. Wobbling a small distance, they sailed toward the opposing wall.

Hugh saw the stone wall approaching. He screamed, and a jarring impact ripped through him. Windchaser had extended his ten-foot-long legs, allowing them to take the impact's brunt. Hugh and Raymond stopped several yards short of colliding with the stone wall.

Windchaser fell back, tried to fly, and struck the wall again with his feet.

Hugh took every blow stoically, though his jaws clattered together and a jarring pain shot through his entire body whenever they hit. His arm ached from clutching Raymond, but he did not let go as they fell again.

They were close to thirty yards from the choppy waters of the canal below when Windchaser dove straight toward a small ledge on the cliffside. The Sky-bax came in for a landing. But the moment weight was placed on the ledge, it collapsed as if it had been made of chalk.

They plunged the rest of the way to the waters, and Windchaser managed to right himself into a semicontrolled glide.

"Donnnn't lllllet Rrrrrayyymonnndddd gggggo!" Windchaser cried as he tried his best to slow them down. Yet they still slapped into the deep waters with a terrible force.

Only a few feet away were a pair of jutting rocks that might have crushed them.

The icy waters of the canal swept over Hugh and Raymond. All three were carried forward, the Skybax struggling to find footing and keep his chest high.

Hugh managed to keep his and Raymond's heads high against Windchaser's upper chest and above the water. But Hugh's torso was still strapped to the Sky-bax's belly. Both he and Raymond might drown before a way to safety could be found.

The waters carried them through a darkened tunnel. They were forced to twist sharply to the right. Suddenly an unexpected brilliance faced them. A white, churning wall of foam loomed.

Hugh saw it first.

"Waterfall!" he cried.

And they were heading right toward it.

CHAPTER 17

Hugh closed his eyes. He held Raymond tight. The strong water currents were tugging at them with more and more force. Their speed seemed to double, then triple, as the roar of the waterfall became louder and louder.

Suddenly there was an odd sensation. A sharp dip. Then they were away from the freezing waters, hanging in midair for a single fleeting instant.

Hugh held his breath, waiting for the certain deadly drop.

Any time now, he thought. *Any time.*

Nothing happened. They were moving, yes, racing forward as if the currents still had hold of them, but they were not falling.

Hugh opened his eyes and looked down. The waterfall was behind them. Its thunderous roar grew softer and softer. Below, he saw the waters branching off into several tributaries. Land was beneath them. Other mountainous rises loomed just ahead.

"Flying," a voice said.

Hugh was so startled he nearly dropped his friend! "Flying," Raymond said again, his voice dreamy.

"Yes," Hugh said, choking back tears. "I'll be a bloody rotter if we're not!"

Looking up, Hugh saw Windchaser as if through Raymond's eyes. The sun was making an appearance. The Skybax's wings no longer seemed damaged. Instead, they seemed aglow with the colors of twilight.

Windchaser was not an object deserving of pity. Hugh now saw his majesty. It was a sight so grand even the most jaded heart would feel new again—and finally come to believe in miracles.

"You're flying!" Hugh cried.

The Skybax let out a squall of triumph.

No, Hugh thought. *Not flying. Sailing. Gliding.* The momentum from the waters must have given Windchaser the added lift he needed.

"Flying," Hugh repeated with wonder.

Suddenly a vine snapped. Hugh gasped as he felt another begin to loosen. The harness Hugh had fashioned with vines was coming apart.

"Down would be good!" Hugh screamed. "Down would be very good indeed!"

They whipped along a mountain pass. Suddenly, they came into full view of trees and lush green grass. Windchaser dove downward.

Hugh's stomach lurched. He hoped he wasn't going to be sick.

Just a little longer, just a little longer, he told himself.

Raymond stirred. "Hurts."

"I know," Hugh said. His arms ached with the weight of Raymond, but his full attention now went to calming his friend. "We'll get help for you soon. Don't worry."

Hugh became aware of the ground reaching up. He drew a sharp breath, and Windchaser managed to slow his glide. They were barely moving now and just a few feet off the ground.

Hugh set Raymond down as carefully as he could. Windchaser rose into the air once more, then landed upright a few yards away. The Skybax leaned forward so Hugh could touch his feet to the ground.

"Faith," he said, snaking out of the harness and racing to his injured friend.

Behind them came a flapping of wings, then a squall. Hugh turned to see Windchaser rise into the air again.

No words were necessary. The Skybax would go and quickly return with help. Windchaser took to the skies with a renewed heart.

"See all the trouble you've caused?" Hugh asked as he knelt beside his friend.

Raymond moaned.

"Oh, right. Now we're supposed to feel sorry for you, is that it?"

"Bloomin' stupid...*git*," Raymond managed to whisper.

"Don't talk about yourself that way," Hugh said. "I won't stand for havin' my friends run down."

Raymond managed a smile before the darkness claimed him once more.

Late that evening, Hugh left the infirmary at Skybax Camp. Raymond had two broken legs along with some bad bumps and bruises, but he was going to be all right. Dinotopia's healers had the situation well under control.

Hugh recalled how Raymond had been brought back to camp. Windchaser had returned with a score of Skybaxes and their riders. They brought a special Skybax harness that was made to carry a wounded man or woman. They set it gently under Raymond, strapped him in, then flew him to safety.

One of the Skybax Riders stayed behind to lead Hugh back to camp on foot. Very little conversation passed between Hugh and the rider. Hugh found he was no longer concerned about what other people thought of him. All he cared about was that his friend would get better.

At camp, Hugh was told that Raymond's legs had been reset and fitted into braces. Raymond had slept through the entire procedure, courtesy of a strange-smelling herb the healers brought with them.

Hugh visited Raymond, sitting at his bedside for close to an hour. Raymond spoke in his sleep. "Teach me. You promised. Want to learn to say more. Soul has what body lacks. You promised!"

Hugh turned and left the infirmary. Another visitor waited outside.

Windchaser.

"He's going to be fine," Hugh said.

The Skybax looked around, wary of anyone who might be within earshot.

"No," Hugh said. "Let me do the talking."

Windchaser stared at him intently.

"It doesn't take a genius or something to figure out why you didn't let the people honor you. All I really had to do was put myself in your place and it all made sense."

An agitated trilling came from the Skybax.

"You felt because you weren't able to save that boy yourself, you didn't deserve to be honored. Well, that's not only stupid, it's selfish."

Windchaser took a step back.

"Mind you, I would have done the same thing. In my way, I think I did. After all, what exactly brought you to the training grounds?"

A strange noise came from the Skybax. It sounded exactly like the horn Hugh had blown in warning as he had raced toward the high wires.

Hugh opened his hands. "He would have died if

you hadn't gone for help. He also would have died if I hadn't brought you with my alarm."

"*Tttellll ottttherrrsss,*" Windchaser said, braving discovery.

"No," Hugh said. "I'll leave that up to you."

The Skybax shuddered.

"I know. You don't want anyone to know you can speak our language. Why does that scare you?"

Windchaser's wings beat anxiously.

"Are you worried everyone will treat you as though you're different? Well, too bloody bad! You are different. So am I. Could your life really get any worse than it is right now?"

"*Yyesssss,*" Windchaser said.

"How?"

"*Coullddddd lllllose ffffrrrienddsss.*"

Hugh laughed. "There's nothing you could do to lose Raymond. And if you're saying you consider me a friend, then, fine, I accept the honor. But it is a turn-around from what you were saying in the gap, when we were making the harness."

"*Afffraiiddd youuuuuu.*"

"Yes. Why?"

"*Turnnn Rayyyymonddd agggainnnsttt meee. Youuuuu neeeed himmm tooooo.*"

Hugh shook his head. "I was jealous. It's true. You also said you didn't like me much."

"*Sorrrrrry.*"

"Don't be. I didn't like you, either."

Windchaser made a disquieting sound, an obvious cry of disapproval.

"You know what they say. If you ever came face to face with someone who was exactly like yourself, you'd probably hate him on sight."

Windchaser nodded.

"Donnn'ttt leeeeeave," Windchaser said, distressed.

"No. I'm not going to run away. I'm going to face up to things for a change.

"How about you? Will you be sticking around, or is it the Sky Galley Caves?"

"Wannnnt toooo sttttayyyyy."

"Good," Hugh said. "Because, quite honestly, I think it would break Raymond's heart if either of us ran off on him again. And you made some kind of promise to him. Teaching him more of your language, from what I could gather."

Hugh thought for a moment, then added, "I wonder what Laegreffon would have said about all this. That's one bloke I really wouldn't mind spending time with, ya know? If he and I were in London together, we'd kick up quite a ruckus!"

Windchaser regarded Hugh quizzically. Suddenly, the Skybax shuddered and made a series of strange racking sounds.

"Here, now!" Hugh said. "Are you laughin' at me?"

"Whhhhhooooooo elllllsse?" Windchaser said.

"And what exactly is so funny?"

"*Lllllaegggreffffonnnn. Nnnnotttt bbbbloke! Tttttri-ccerattopsssss!*"

Hugh's jaw gaped open. It took him several moments to compose himself. "He's a *dinosaur?*"

Before Hugh could say anything else on the matter, Raymond's instructor suddenly appeared. Hikaro seemed intent on visiting his student in the infirmary. He looked to Hugh and Windchaser and gave a slight bow.

"My thanks for saving Raymond's life," Hikaro said. "*Doomo arigatoo.*"

The teacher was about to turn away when Windchaser crowded before him. Hikaro stroked Windchaser's flank, as he might any other anxious mount. "Do not worry. Breathe deep. Seek peace." Windchaser shook violently, causing Hikaro to gracefully withdraw.

The teacher looked to Hugh and asked, "What's wrong?"

"I don't know," Hugh said. "Ask him."

Hikaro frowned. "I have no time for games."

Windchaser poked his massive head between the two humans and let out a sound that caused Hikaro to blanch.

"The Skybax just cursed me in my own language!" Hikaro said, astounded. "Or—that's what it sounded like."

"He isn't always in the best of moods, I'll admit," Hugh said.

"How very odd," Hikaro said, turning his back on the Skybax.

"*Wwwwwhere wwwwere yourrrrr ppppeople?*" Windchaser asked.

Hikaro turned slowly, this time with a slight flush of anger playing on his cheeks. "Parlor tricks such as ventriloquism are amusing in their time and place, young man, but this is hardly—"

"*Lllllisstennnn!*" Windchaser cried in a voice no human could ever duplicate.

Hikaro's eyes widened.

"He talks," Hugh said. "In his way."

"Does he, now?" Hikaro asked, his tone changing to one of astonished interest.

"*Hughhhh ssssssounnnnnded alllarm wwhhennn boyyyy felll. Yyourrrr ottherrr sssstudennntsss shhhould hhhhave ccommme. Theyyy wwwerre offfff playyying. Lllllaughhhing. Mmmmakking nnooise. I sawwww themmmm. Theyyyy nnnnever hearrrrrd. Onnnnly I diddddd. Hhhhhhughhh nnnnottt baddddd. Dolllphinnns rrrighttt aboutt himmm.*"

Hikaro nodded somberly. "Yes, I see now. I did not reason this out. My ancestors would be ashamed of how I allowed my emotions to overcome me. Hugh, please forgive me. The other students will be chastised. And at the next celebration—"

"No," Hugh said. "It's done and in the past. If there's anything worth celebrating, it's what Windchaser is doing—talking!"

Hikaro nodded and stared at the great creature before him. "Windchaser, I can see many ways for you to help the people of Dinotopia. The question is, are you up to the challenge? Are you willing to try?"

"You can do this," Hugh encouraged the worried Skybax.

Nodding, the Skybax performed yet another act of true bravery. *"I wwwilllll!"*

EPILOGUE

Several months passed. The strange herbs of the island helped Raymond to recover from his injuries with astounding speed. He was now up and walking about with only a small amount of pain.

The younger boy learned that he had lost his father's pocketwatch during his trials in the Forbidden Mountains.

"You don't need it," said Hugh. "You never did. If you want to see something of your father, just look in the mirror."

Those words meant a great deal to Raymond. They also helped him to make a very important decision.

Raymond and Hugh traveled to Canyon City, looking for their closest friend. They enjoyed a brief tour of this magnificent place. Carved out of the stone canyon walls, Canyon City overlooked a deep gorge and served as the center of all Skybax Rider training. In fact, the city sat so high, the residents had the pleasure of living among both clouds and rainbows.

After seeing many of the breathtaking views the city offered, they were shown into the courtyard of a grand building. There Windchaser stood between two delegations—one made up of humans and Saurians, the other one of Skybaxes.

Because Windchaser was the first Skybax to understand human and Saurian languages, he had been appointed the honored task of acting as a translator and liaison.

The conference ended, and Windchaser turned to greet his friends. *"Breeathe deeeep! Seeeek peaccccce!"*

Raymond was about to speak when Hugh, glowing like a proud older brother, cut him off.

"Have you heard?" Hugh asked. "Raymond is going to become a healer!"

"Yyouuuu hhonorr yourrr fffather's mmemorrryyy!"

"He's also got quite a talent on his own!" Hugh said. "Look at what he did for the two of us."

Windchaser nodded. The Skybax finally seemed at peace. *"Annndddd Huuuugh?"*

Raymond jumped in this time. "Sollis has sent word to Laegreffon. Hugh is going to study philosophy with the diplomat and perhaps write some words of wisdom of his own!"

Windchaser nodded approvingly.

Hugh said, "I've spent my life worrying about the future. I've always seen it as bleak. Now I see nothing before me except possibilities."

"Sssseconddd channnncesss!"

"Yes," Hugh said. For the first time in his life, he saw the future as glorious and far-reaching as the grandest vistas of Canyon City. And it held just as many unexplored possibilities!

"I don't know where I'll end up, or what I'll be doing," said Hugh. "Perhaps I will become a diplomat like Laegreffon. Or something else may come my way. That's not really important. It's the journey that matters, not the destination."

"There's more," Raymond said, placing his hand on Hugh's shoulder.

Hugh smiled and nodded. So much more. Like friendship and love, which Dinotopia possessed in abundance—the very qualities that made life's journeys worth the taking.

"It doesn't matter where I am on this island," Hugh said. "For the first time in my life, I'm home."